The Thanksgiving Trip

by

Kathi Daley

This book is a work of fiction. Names, characters, places, and incidents either are products of the author's imagination or are used fictitiously. Any resemblance to actual events or locales or persons, living or dead, is entirely coincidental.

I want to thank the very talented Jessica Fischer for the cover art.

I so appreciate Bruce Curran, who is always ready and willing to answer my cyber questions; Jayme Maness for helping out with the book clubs; and Peggy Hyndman for helping sleuth out those pesky typos.

And, of course, thanks to the readers and bloggers in my life, who make doing what I do possible.

Thank you to Randy Ladenheim-Gil for the editing.

And finally, I want to thank my husband Ken for allowing me time to write by taking care of everything else.

Books by Kathi Daley
Come for the murder, stay for the romance.

Zoe Donovan Cozy Mystery:
Halloween Hijinks
The Trouble With Turkeys
Christmas Crazy
Cupid's Curse
Big Bunny Bump-off
Beach Blanket Barbie
Maui Madness
Derby Divas
Haunted Hamlet
Turkeys, Tuxes, and Tabbies
Christmas Cozy
Alaskan Alliance
Matrimony Meltdown
Soul Surrender
Heavenly Honeymoon
Hopscotch Homicide
Ghostly Graveyard
Santa Sleuth
Shamrock Shenanigans
Kitten Kaboodle
Costume Catastrophe
Candy Cane Caper
Holiday Hangover
Easter Escapade
Camp Carter
Trick or Treason
Reindeer Roundup
Hippity Hoppity Homicide

Firework Fiasco
Henderson House
Holiday Hostage – *December 2017*

Zimmerman Academy The New Normal
Zimmerman Academy New Beginnings
Ashton Falls Cozy Cookbook

Tj Jensen Paradise Lake Mysteries by Henery Press:

Pumpkins in Paradise
Snowmen in Paradise
Bikinis in Paradise
Christmas in Paradise
Puppies in Paradise
Halloween in Paradise
Treasure in Paradise
Fireworks in Paradise
Beaches in Paradise
Thanksgiving in Paradise – *fall 2019*

Whales and Tails Cozy Mystery:

Romeow and Juliet
The Mad Catter
Grimm's Furry Tail
Much Ado About Felines
Legend of Tabby Hollow
Cat of Christmas Past
A Tale of Two Tabbies
The Great Catsby
Count Catula
The Cat of Christmas Present
A Winter's Tail

The Taming of the Tabby
Frankencat
The Cat of Christmas Future
Farewell to Felines
A Whisker in Time
The Catsgiving Feast – *November 2018*

Writers' Retreat Southern Seashore Mystery:

First Case
Second Look
Third Strike
Fourth Victim
Fifth Night
Sixth Cabin
Seventh Chapter

Rescue Alaska Paranormal Mystery:

Finding Justice
Finding Answers
Finding Courage
Finding Christmas – *December 2018*

A Tess and Tilly Mystery:

The Christmas Letter
The Valentine Mystery
The Mother's Day Mishap
The Halloween House
The Thanksgiving Trip

The Inn at Holiday Bay:
Boxes in the Basement – *November 2018*

Haunting by the Sea:
Homecoming by the Sea
Secrets by the Sea
Missing by the Sea
Christmas by the Sea – *December 2018*

Sand and Sea Hawaiian Mystery:
Murder at Dolphin Bay
Murder at Sunrise Beach
Murder at the Witching Hour
Murder at Christmas
Murder at Turtle Cove
Murder at Water's Edge
Murder at Midnight

Seacliff High Mystery:
The Secret
The Curse
The Relic
The Conspiracy
The Grudge
The Shadow
The Haunting

Road to Christmas Romance:
Road to Christmas Past

Chapter 1

Friday, November 16

"Morning, Hap," I said to Hap Hollister as my dog Tilly and I entered his home and hardware store to deliver his mail.

"Mornin', Tess; Tilly. Are you all set for your trip?"

I nodded. "We are. When my mom first suggested that we head up to Timberland Lake for Thanksgiving, I wasn't sure that was what I wanted to do. But Mom seems to really want to go, and with Aunt Ruthie at Johnny's for the holiday, they decided to close the restaurant from this Sunday until the Monday after Thanksgiving. It seemed like a good opportunity, and I hated to have her waste her time off."

Hap ran a hand through his thick white hair. "Sounds like it might be fun. Is Tony going with you?"

"He is. I have an adoption clinic tomorrow, and Mom and Aunt Ruthie plan to be open as well, so we're all heading out on Sunday morning."

"Mike going as well?" Hap asked as he began to sort through the stack of mail I'd left on his counter.

"Actually, he is. He got Frank to cover for him, so he has the whole week off." My brother, Mike Thomas, is a police officer right here in White Eagle, Montana, and Frank Hudson is his partner. "Bree is closing the bookstore and coming with us, so I imagine we'll have a nice time. Are you going to Hattie's for the holiday?" Hattie Johnson was Hap's wife, or ex-wife, or something. I wasn't exactly sure about the details. What I did know was that they used to be married and lived together and now they didn't live together, but they did date.

"Yup. Hattie's planning a traditional meal with all the fixin's. Should have enough leftovers to last several days at least."

"That's what I love about Thanksgiving. All the leftovers. Do you have any outgoing mail?"

Hap nodded. "Hang on, I'll get it."

I walked over to Hap's woodburning stove to warm up while I waited. We'd had a cold November so far, as well as several snow showers. I had to admit I had a few reservations about heading up to Timberland Lake despite what I'd said to Hap. Not that I wasn't looking forward to cuddling up by the fire with my boyfriend, Tony Marconi, but Timberland Lake was the same place where my dad went fishing alone every fall, and I had to wonder why, out of all the possible vacation spots, my mom had picked that specific one to have our family holiday. To be honest, ever since I found out my dad was most likely not dead, as we'd all believed for years, I'd been questioning a lot of things.

"Here you go." Hap handed me a stack of mail. "I'm going to miss your sunny face next week, but I hope you have a wonderful time."

"Thanks, Hap. And I hope you and Hattie have a wonderful holiday as well."

After Tilly and I left Hap's store, we continued down the street, dropping off mail and pausing to chat with the people we met along the way. I really love my job. Not that I'd lay awake at night when I was a child dreaming of life as a mail carrier for the US Postal Service, but delivering the daily mail to the merchants in White Eagle gave me the opportunity to stay current with the local news *and* the local gossip.

Not that I couldn't have stayed up-to-date by hanging out in the restaurant my mom owned and operated with my Aunt Ruthie, but there was something pretty perfect about being outdoors in the fresh air for most of the day. I glanced up at the dark clouds overhead. Well, at least it was usually nice to be outdoors. I had to admit that when the cold Montana winter took hold, there were days I found myself wishing I'd been a hairdresser, a florist, or even a podiatrist.

"Morning, Bree," I greeted my best friend, Bree Price, who also happened to be Mike's girlfriend. "The store looks fantastic."

"Thanks. I figured the Christmas rush will have started by the time we return from our trip, so I wanted to have all the decorating taken care of before I left."

"I love the little Victorian village. It's so quaint and perfect. Very bookish."

Bree smiled. "I like it. I got the idea from your mom. The Santa's Village she sets up in the restaurant every year is adorable. I wanted to do something similar yet smaller, with a Dickens feel. I'm also going to put a tree in the corner I cleared out near the front door. I want a fresh tree, not a fake, so I figured I'd cut one down while we're up at the lake. When people ask where I got it, I'll have a story to go with the tree."

"I'm pretty sure Tony is bringing his truck, although we do have two dogs and two cats to transport. Let's make sure Mike brings his truck too. He has a back seat, so you can bring Mom with you. We'll have cat carriers on our back seat."

Bree continued to hang the white twinkle lights she'd been stringing around the store when I walked in. "I'm excited about the trip. I've never been to Timberland Lake, but I hear it's beautiful."

"I've never been either," I answered. "In fact, I don't think any of us have, so it'll be a new experience all around."

"I wonder why your mom chose that specific lake if she'd never been there," Bree mused.

"My dad used to go up there every year. I guess he must have told her about it."

Bree's smile faded. "Maybe she's missing him."

I paused. "Maybe. Although he's been gone for a long time. I have a feeling there's something else behind her desire to rent a cabin at that lake, although I have no idea what it is."

Bree shrugged. "I don't suppose it really matters. A cabin at the lake sounds like the perfect place to spend a good old-fashioned Thanksgiving."

"It does sound relaxing," I agreed.

"I have a couple of new holiday-themed mysteries that arrived today. They won't even officially be on sale until after Thanksgiving, but I nabbed us a couple. I'll grab one for your mom as well. Maybe we can all read the same book and then hold a discussion."

"Sounds like a lot of work for a vacation."

"It'll be fun."

I groaned. While Bree found reading relaxing, I much preferred a video game. Not that I never read. I did. But I was a slow reader, and I didn't want the extra burden of reading so many pages a day in order to participate in a discussion.

Bree and I chatted for a few more minutes, then Tilly and I continued on our way. I wanted to take a minute to chat with everyone as I dropped off the mail so I could remind them that they'd have a substitute mail carrier the following week, but I also wanted to finish my route at a decent time. Tony was coming over for dinner and gaming tonight, and I wanted to get home in time to clean up a bit before he arrived. Not that it mattered all that much if I didn't manage to get my laundry tucked away in the hamper. I was sure Tony loved me, messy home and all.

"Afternoon, Brick," I said to local pub owner Brick Brannigan. "You have mail today." I held up two envelopes. Brick didn't have mail more than once or sometimes twice a week, so I didn't come in every day, as I did with the other merchants on Main.

Brick reached out a hand. "Thanks. I've been waiting for a letter from my uncle, who's coming into town next week. I still don't know what day to expect him."

"Why don't you just text or email him?"

"He doesn't do cell phones or texts or emails. He's currently on a road trip, so I can't call him on his landline. He said he'd drop me a letter once he'd narrowed things down to a specific date." Brick ripped open one of the envelopes. He took a minute to read whatever was handwritten on the enclosed piece of paper. "It looks like he'll be here Wednesday."

"That's good." I smiled. "He'll be with you for Thanksgiving."

Brick frowned. "Yeah, but then I'll have to cook. Maybe I'll just take him to your mom's place."

"She's closing the restaurant for the whole week. I think pretty much everyone's closed on Thanksgiving Day. Maybe you can buy a precooked turkey from the meat market and add a few sides. Actually, you might be able to buy the sides precooked as well."

"Good idea. I'll do that."

I'd turned to leave when Jordan Westlake walked in. Jordan was new to White Eagle. He'd moved to town the previous month after inheriting an old house he was in the process of renovating. It was huge, so the renovation was going to take some time, but I couldn't wait to see what he'd done with the place so far.

"Afternoon, Tess," Jordan greeted.

"Afternoon, Jordan. How's the renovation going?"

"Pretty well. The kitchen is just about done, as is one of the bathrooms on the first floor. I have a long way to go, but I finally feel like the place is functional."

"I can't wait to see what you've done with the house. It really does have so much potential, and when we discussed your plans, they sounded wonderful."

"It's been a labor of love, although love isn't the only emotion I've felt for the place."

"That's understandable after everything that happened there. I heard you went to visit Hannah and Houston last week." Hannah and Houston Harrington were twins and Jordan's cousins. Sort of. It's a long story, but basically, Hannah and Houston spent two years living in the house Jordan now owned after their father dumped them, along with their three other siblings, in White Eagle while he went on with his life in San Francisco. The legend surrounding the house had been both creepy and incomplete, so Tony and I, along with Mike and Bree, had helped Jordan track down the truth, which led to the information that the two youngest of the Harrington siblings hadn't died as teens as everyone had thought after all.

Jordan nodded. "I did go to visit them."

"And how was it?"

"Strange, but nice. I felt a little weird to be the one who ended up with the house, even though I'm not a Harrington by blood. It does seem the house should have gone to one or both of them, but they assured me that they were fine with my having it because neither had any intention of returning to it or White Eagle ever again."

I understood that. Their time in White Eagle had been its own kind of hell.

Jordan continued. "I'm happy to be able to confirm that both Hannah and Houston have gone on to have fairly normal and happy lives. They most definitely had a rough start, but once they got out from under their father's control they seem to have blossomed."

"I'm really happy to hear that. Any news on Hillary?" Hillary was Hannah and Houston's older sister. She'd run away long before they did.

"I haven't had any luck tracking her down. I have a feeling the twins know where she's been since her disappearance, and whether she's still alive now, but it was very apparent that, while they were interested in meeting me, the subject of their sister was off the table."

"If they do know where she's been, and if she's still alive, I imagine they're protecting her. It's a complicated situation."

"It really is. I have plans to see them again. I think we can be a family of sorts. I'm hoping over time they'll be willing to fill in the blanks about Hillary."

"I hope so. It would be nice to have the rest of the story."

"It really would. I'm heading to San Francisco next week to spend Thanksgiving with family, but I'd love to get together with you and Tony when I get back."

"Call me and we'll set up a date. Maybe for dinner."

"Sounds good, as long as we go out or you're planning to do the cooking. I'm afraid that isn't one of my talents."

"Tony's an excellent cook. I'll invite Mike and Bree too, and we'll meet up at his place. Feel free to bring a date, or if you don't know anyone, I can invite someone to even things out."

"I have someone in mind," Jordan said. "I'll call you when I get back."

I said goodbye to Brick and continued on my route. It looked like Tony was going to have to live with socks and underwear on the floor. I should have done the picking up in the morning, but I'd gotten a late start and really did think I'd have time to get to it this afternoon. I sighed. Oh well; there were worse things than a messy cabin.

I was just finishing up when I got a call from Brady Baker, the veterinarian in town. About a year ago, Brady had taken over for his uncle, who had been the only vet in White Eagle for a long time. In addition to running the veterinary clinic, Brady owned and operated an animal shelter.

"Oh good, I caught you," Brady said. "I wanted to ask if you could come to the clinic early tomorrow morning."

"Sure. I can do that. Is something up?" I opened the door to my Jeep and Tilly jumped inside. I tossed my empty mailbag on the back seat.

"There's a man coming by at seven thirty to look at three of our dogs. He adopts dogs from shelters around the country and trains them for FEMA. He's in our area and heard about our shelter. He was impressed with our personalized training program and asked if I thought we had any dogs with potential. I want to show him Gracie, Bosley, and Sammy. I hoped you could be here to help me with the demonstration."

"I'm happy to help out. What a great opportunity." Gracie was a golden lab, Bosley a German shepherd, and Sammy a Border collie mix. All had received basic training and were young and healthy. I considered them to have real potential for specialized training as search-and-rescue dogs.

"Great. I'll see you in the morning. And bring Tilly. She has a calming effect on the shelter dogs."

By the time I dropped off my empty mailbag and chatted with my coworker for a few minutes at the post office, it was a good thirty minutes past the time Tony had told me he'd be by. I'd given him a key to my cabin and knew he'd let himself in, but I'd hoped to be home early enough not to keep him waiting. Our lives had certainly changed since we'd admitted our love for each other. I felt like the world around me was somehow brighter, richer, and happier. I'm not sure why I hadn't realized sooner that Tony was the guy for me, but now that I'd opened my eyes, I planned to never let him go.

Tony's truck was in the drive when I pulled up. He'd turned on the white twinkle lights he'd strung all around my property, making it look like a magical fairyland. My heart smiled as I climbed out of my Jeep and let Tilly out behind me. "Titan's here," I said to Tilly, referring to Tony's dog.

Tilly must have figured that out on her own because she ran toward the front door the minute I let her out of the Jeep. Tilly loved Titan, and it was obvious the feeling was mutual.

Tony opened the door and stepped out onto the front deck. I walked into his arms and sighed with happiness when they closed around me. Tony had been working hard to finish up a project he'd contracted for and wanted to have completed before we left for our trip, so I hadn't seen him since the previous Monday morning, when he'd brought me back to my cabin after we'd spent the weekend at his place.

"I've missed you," Tony said into my ear.

"And I've missed you. Did you finish your project?"

"I did. And I don't have anything else until after the first of the year, so from this point forward, I'm all yours."

"That sounds pretty darn good to me."

Tony took a step back and we turned toward the front door. "I was about to start dinner," he informed me.

"It can wait. I need to change out of my uniform and I thought maybe you could help me."

Tony grinned. "You know I like to be helpful."

******

A long time later, Tony started dinner, while I logged onto my computer to check my emails. I didn't normally get a lot, but I didn't have time to check them at all during the day, so I'd settled into the routine of checking all my messages when I got home each evening. I supposed missing an evening wouldn't be the end of the world, but ever since Tony and I had begun searching for my father, I felt compelled to check to see if I'd received anything that might be connected to it in some way. Not that I ever had. The only email we'd received that was even remotely connected to it was one Tony had received about my mother. Still, although the clues leading to my dad's disappearance were slim, a girl could dream.

I thought about the information we'd been able to uncover as I waited for the computer to boot up. The whole thing had started shortly after my dad died, or I should say supposedly died, fourteen years ago. I was fourteen when I was told my dad had died in a fiery truck accident while driving the cross-country route he'd been working most of my life. A year later, I was nosing around in the attic of the house Mike and I lived in with our mother and found a letter hidden in a book that I believed at the time to be encrypted. Believing it could somehow provide an answer to the questions I'd been having since my father's death, I'd decided to try to break the code. After dozens of failed attempts, I had no choice but to enlist Tony's help. As it turned out, the letter hadn't been encrypted at all, but that search had led us to uncover some anomalies in my father's death, which was what I'd suspected all along. We decided to keep our search to ourselves as we continued to dig. We'd come up totally empty until this past December, when Tony found a photo of my dad standing in front of a building that had been constructed three years after his supposed death. Two months after that, Tony found a photo of my dad in a minimart. At the time, the photo had been only two years old.

Since then, we'd gotten other hits that suggested my dad was not only alive but something of a world traveler. We hadn't been able to find mention of a Grant Thomas since his death, so we were working under the assumption that he'd changed his name. The most recent clue was a photo sent to Tony just three weeks ago. That photo of my dad looked as if it had been taken in Eastern Europe and appeared to come to him in real time, meaning that unless it was a trick of some sort, my dad was alive as of three weeks ago. Of course, Tony had warned me the photo could be a fake, and we should consider any evidence we dug up suspect until proven otherwise.

The other interesting thing Tony had uncovered was that Grant Walton Thomas didn't seem to exist before 1981. As far as I knew, he was born on April 12, 1957, in St. Louis, Missouri, but according to Tony, he didn't have a paper trail of any sort until shortly before he married my mother.

In addition to the photos of my dad that Tony had dug up along the way, someone had sent him a photo of my mom standing on a bridge in Norway. I later learned that was taken while she was on vacation in Europe before she ever met my father. The really odd thing was, in the photo she's standing on the same bridge as the man we thought could have been my father at an earlier age. I spoke to Mom about it, and she assured me that, while they did look alike, Jared Collins, the man on the bridge, and my father weren't the same man.

The more we learned about my father's past and disappearance, the more confused I became. I wondered who had sent Tony the photo of my mom and why. It wasn't as if we were doing a facial recognition search on her image, so why had the photo turned up in his in-box?

"Because I've barely spoken to you in a week, I wanted to ask if you had any new hits on my dad," I said after I'd checked my handful of emails—mostly ads—and logged off.

Tony paused from chopping garlic. "I haven't had any additional hits with the facial recognition program, but I've done some digging to see if I can turn up anything connected to your dad's time at Timberland Lake. When you told me that your mom wanted us to spend the week at the place your dad took his annual fishing trip, I decided to look for any references I might be able to uncover."

"Makes sense."

"Did your mom happen to say why she wanted to visit that particular lake?"

I shook my head. "I thought it odd that she wanted to go there after all these years when she first brought it up, but I didn't want to make a big deal out of it so I didn't say anything."

"Do you think it might have something to do with your asking her about her trip to Europe last month?"

I frowned. "Maybe. I guess that would explain why she's suddenly interested in visiting a place my dad spent so much time during their marriage. Bree wondered if Mom missed Dad and was looking to make a connection of some sort by visiting a place he seemed to love so much."

"Do you think she's right? Do you think she's missing your dad?"

"I don't think so. That doesn't feel right to me. She loved my dad, but it wasn't the stuff of fairy tales. They actually didn't spend a lot of time together. He was on the road most of the time, and even when he wasn't working, he would go fishing or hunting. And yes, she was sad when he died, but I don't remember her falling into a deep depression. In fact, it seemed to me that she grieved quickly and then got on with her life in a fairly efficient manner. To suggest she'd be missing him all these years later would be odd. I suspect she might just want to do something different this year. Aunt Ruthie is going to be out of town with her son and new granddaughter. Mom might just have been feeling at loose ends."

Tony tossed the garlic he'd chopped into a pan with diced onions and olive oil, then began to stir. "I guess that might be all there is going on. Still, it seems like a good opportunity for us to dig up a new clue. I don't think we should be obvious about it, but I do think we should plan to do a little sleuthing while we're at the lake. If your dad went up there every year, I'd be willing to bet there are people who live in the area who might remember him."

I popped a piece of the bread Tony had buttered in preparation for broiling into my mouth. "That's a good idea. The fact that he returned to the same lake every year with such faithfulness almost makes me think he was meeting someone there."

"Did he ever mention seeing anyone?" Tony asked.

"No. He just said he needed time to think," I answered. "That never made sense to me because he spent most of his time driving back and forth across the country alone. Seems like he had plenty of time to think then. But my mom seemed fine with it, so who was I to question his motives?"

"My research turned up the fact that the man who owns and rents the cabins on the lake has been doing it for over thirty years. He must have known your dad. And if he was meeting someone there, he should know that as well. As soon as we get settled, we'll head over to the rental office and have a chat with the guy."

I frowned as a thought occurred to me. "If my dad is still alive, which we seem to have good reason to suspect he is, do you think he continued to go up to the lake even after he supposedly died?"

Tony tossed some shrimp into the sauté. "I wouldn't think he would have. I mean, he was supposed to be dead. It seems like he'd go out of his way to avoid any place where he was known in his old life."

"Yeah. I guess you're right. But how funny would it be to run into him by the lake or at the local pub?"

Chapter 2

Sunday, November 18

"The man who adopts dogs to train for FEMA ended up taking all three of the dogs we showed him yesterday," I said to Tony as we drove toward the cabin on the lake where we would spend the next week.

"That's wonderful. And I love the idea that he uses rescue dogs for his program."

I turned to look at Tilly and Titan, who were riding comfortably in the cargo area of the new SUV Tony had bought after we'd discussed the fact that carting two dogs and two cats up to the lake in a truck was going to be tricky. "Rescue dogs are the best. The three we showed him had undergone quite a bit of training already, so I was really optimistic things would work out."

"I think it's wonderful that you and Brady put so much time into training the dogs in your care."

"Most dogs who end up in the shelter are brought to us in the first place because they have bad habits the owners can't tolerate. Brady and I know that well-behaved dogs are more likely to be well-loved dogs, so we're willing to go the extra mile. Our goal is to place our animals in forever homes, not just more temporary ones. So far, I think we've had really good luck."

"Well, I certainly adore Titan. I never even knew I wanted a dog until you brought him to me. Now I can't imagine life without him." Tony turned to me. "Or without you."

I smiled.

"How are the cats doing?" he asked.

My cats, Tang and Tinder, were in crates on the back seat, with the luggage tied onto the roof rack. "They don't seem to be loving the long ride, but they're hanging in okay. How much farther do you think it is?"

"At least another hour."

I turned back around and glanced at the truck in front of us. As we'd discussed, Mike and Bree had taken Mom and her luggage, and all the food and supplies she'd brought. We'd discussed cutting a tree for Bree while at the lake, but I wasn't sure we'd have the space to bring it home. Of course, by the time we made the return trip, the boxes of food would be gone, which would free up some room.

"It really is beautiful up here," I said as we wound our way up the mountain. "And so peaceful. I guess I can see why Dad wanted to come up here every year."

"My research indicated the cabins as well as the campgrounds are packed in the summer, but the campground is closed from mid-September through mid-May, so there shouldn't be a lot of activity at this time of the year."

"Once we arrive, we'll get the cats settled, then take the dogs for a walk," I said. "I'm sure they'll need to stretch their legs."

"I could use a walk as well," Tony agreed.

"I'm curious to see how populated the place actually is. I've been picturing a little town perched on the edge of a lake with cabins scattered around, but the map Mom has makes it look really isolated."

"I have the feeling it's pretty isolated. In fact, there didn't seem to be a town of any sort in the vicinity of the lake, but there's a little one about ten miles away. If I had to guess, that serves as a place to eat and shop for the folks staying in the cabins and campground at the lake."

"Mom said she thought the lake had a small café and store."

"Makes sense. I think the road we need to turn on to is coming up within the next few miles. We should start to watch for it."

I narrowed my gaze to focus on the road ahead. I pointed to an intersection in the distance. "I think that might be it just ahead."

Mike slowed and made the turn, and Tony followed him.

"It looks like Mike is pulling over," I said after we'd both left the interstate and merged onto the lake road.

Tony pulled over behind him.

Mike made a complete stop and got out of the truck. Tony and I followed suit.

"What's going on?" I asked.

Mike pointed toward a grove of aspens. "When we made the turn, there was a pup in the road. I didn't hit him, but I did scare him. He took off toward those trees."

I looked around. There didn't seem to be a house in sight. "We should try to get him. We can take him with us. I'm sure someone at the lake will know who he belongs to."

"I'll get him," Mike said.

Tony and I waited to see if he was successful. If he wasn't, I'd get Tilly out of Tony's SUV to see if the pup would come to her. We didn't have to wait long until Mike came back out of the trees with a tan and white bundle of fur who was wagging his tail and licking Mike's face.

"It seems he likes you," I said.

"Apparently," Mike grumbled. "Let's put him in the cargo area of your vehicle with Tilly and Titan. I don't think Mom is going to want to share the back seat with him."

"You're probably right." I opened the cargo area and Mike slipped the pup inside. He seemed to be thrilled to join Tilly and Titan, so we closed the back door, and Mike returned to his truck.

"The pup can't be more than a few months old," Tony commented as we resumed the drive.

I frowned. "Yeah. He's much too young to be out on his own. I wonder where he came from."

"He's pretty darn cute and friendly. I'd say he was a stray, but he seems as if he's used to people. Maybe he wandered away from one of the cabins."

"Maybe. I'm glad Mike saw him. He shouldn't be out here on his own." I turned and looked at the pup, who was resting his paws on the back seat. His tongue hung out to the side and his entire body was wiggling with excitement as he spotted the cats. "You need to stay in the back," I warned the pup. "I don't think the cats are happy to have you drooling on them."

The pup ignored me, but he didn't continue over the seat either. We had to be close to the lake by now, so I decided to just keep an eye on him rather than stopping to secure him.

"There's more snow up here than I was expecting," Tony commented as we continued to climb toward the lake. "If I'd known, I would have brought my cross-country skis."

I glanced at the dark sky. "It looks like we might be in for some additional snow while we're here. Skiing would have been fun, but it will also be fun to snuggle up by the fire and watch it snow."

Tony grabbed my hand and gave it a squeeze. "Suddenly, I'm wishing we had our own cabin."

I squeezed Tony's hand in return. "That would be romantic, but I think for Mom, this weekend is about family, and that should be nice too. She's planning to cook up a storm, which will be wonderful. And she brought cards, puzzles, and board games."

Tony slowed the SUV. "It looks like Mike is getting ready to make a turn."

I watched as both vehicles left the little mountain road and turned onto a narrow lane that seemed to be more of a service road. It wasn't long before the lake came into view. My breath caught in my throat as I took in the natural beauty of the area. "Wow," I said aloud.

"Wow is right," Tony said. "It's gorgeous."

The large lake was surrounded by dense forest. Cabins, both large and small, were scattered along the shoreline. It appeared as if there was a one-lane road that circled the lake, providing access to the cabins. At the south end was a larger complex that included, as Mom had suggested, a large cabin, I assume belonging to the owner, a one-pump gas station, a camp store, a laundry, and a small café, which was closed. I wasn't sure if that was because it was Sunday or if it was closed for the season. Not that it mattered. Mom had brought plenty of supplies to cook up several feasts.

Mike pulled up in front of the camp store and parked, and we followed. Mike, Bree, and Mom all climbed out of the truck, and so did we.

"It's freezing," I said as we exited the warm interior of the truck.

"Do you want me to dig out your jacket?" Tony asked.

I rubbed my hands up and down my arms. "No, I'm fine. I imagine this is where you check in. Once Mom gets the keys, we can head to the cabin and unpack."

The five of us entered the little store, which was well stocked for such a small enterprise. Mom gave the man behind the counter her name, and he produced a set of keys and a map. I wandered around, looking at the various items for sale, while Mike and Mom got directions to our cabin. I was happy to see the store carried all the staples one might need, including eggs, milk, bread, butter, and flour. I couldn't help but notice the rows of chips, candy, and other junk food too. I guess I was hungry. It had been a long time since breakfast.

"We're all set," Mike said as he walked up to me. "We're on the opposite end of the lake. There's a one-way road that will take us there. Do you need anything while we're here?"

"Maybe some chips." I grabbed a bag. "I'm starving."

"Okay. We'll head out to the truck while you pay for those."

I purchased my chips and Tony and I got back into his SUV. The one-way road was narrow, so the going was slow. After puttering along at five miles an hour for a good ten or fifteen minutes, Mike pulled up in front of a two-story house. Beyond it was a large deck, and beyond that a dock, which would be great in the summertime.

"Wow, this is really nice," I said. It was so quiet and peaceful. A lot like home, but different as well.

"Let's get this stuff unloaded and then we can take the dogs for a walk before the sun goes down," Tony suggested.

I opened the tailgate, and all three dogs jumped down. Of course, as was required of any new location, the dogs ran around sniffing at and peeing on everything in sight. I kept my eye on them as Tony carried the cat carriers into the house. We'd decided we'd let the cats out in our bedroom, with food, water, and a cat box, while the rest of the supplies were being unloaded. Once they got used to the room, and the vehicles were unloaded and the front door could be closed, I'd introduce them to the rest of the house.

"We have a fireplace in our room," Tony said when he came back outside. "In fact, the house has four suites, all with attached baths and fireplaces. The main living area has a huge rock fireplace that's almost two stories high. When you said your mom had rented a cabin at the lake, I was visualizing something a lot more rustic."

"Me too," I said. "I wonder why Mom got such a big place. It must be costing her a fortune."

Tony leaned over and kissed my neck. "I guess she realized privacy might be an issue with five adults living together for a week. Our room is on the second floor. If you want to check it out or need to use the facilities, I can keep an eye on the dogs."

"Thanks. I would like to check on the cats."

"Just take a left at the top of the stairs. There are two suites on each floor. We have the second-story suite to the left and Mike and Bree have the one to the right. Your mom is on the first floor."

I jogged into the house, found our room, checked on the cats, used the bathroom, then grabbed my jacket from the suitcase someone had dropped off. I headed back out to the hallway, where I ran into Bree.

"Isn't this fabulous?" she asked.

"It is pretty spectacular," I agreed. "I had no idea Mom had rented such a nice place."

"There's even a hot tub on the back deck. And the kitchen. Did you see the kitchen?"

"Not yet."

"It's fabulous. When your mom said she planned to cook a full Thanksgiving dinner with all the trimmings, I wondered how she would pull that off in a cabin in the woods. But the kitchen is not only huge, the appliances look almost new."

"It does seem larger and newer than any of the other cabins. I suppose the man who owns the land might have wanted to start catering to larger groups."

"I guess that makes sense. It would be a nice place to have a family reunion or a corporate retreat."

I looked toward the stairs. "Tony and I are going to take the dogs for a walk before it gets dark. I didn't see where Mom went, but if you could let her know we'll be back in an hour, that would be appreciated."

"Sure. No problem. Have fun."

Tony and I both changed into our heavy boots and donned our heavy jackets, then set off along the lake trail with the three dogs. It appeared the pup had settled in just fine. I'd overheard Mike asking the man at the general store when we'd checked in if anyone was missing a puppy. Not that he knew of, he'd said, but he'd ask around and let us know if he heard anything. I'd also overheard him tell Mike that most of the cabins were vacant now, the café was closed until spring, and the little store was only open a few hours a day, from noon until four. During the winter, it was closed most Sundays and Mondays too, but he'd opened today because he knew we were checking in.

I'm sure the lake was a fun place to be when the cabins were full and there were boats on the water, but I was just as happy for the quiet. "This is really nice," I said to Tony as we walked hand in hand behind the dogs. "I can see why my dad came up here every year."

"It's a beautiful location. And a lot more isolated than I expected. The little cabins around the lake seem just right, but the big cabin your mom rented seems somewhat out of place."

"It's certainly larger and newer than anything else here. Bree and I wondered if it might have been added to accommodate larger groups."

"Makes sense."

Titan came running back to Tony and me with something in his mouth. It wasn't the stick Tony had thrown but a hat. A baseball cap. "Where did you get that?" I asked the German shepherd as I looked around for Tilly and the pup, who seemed to have disappeared. "Tilly," I called. My call was met with barking. "Come on back."

Tilly came running toward me from a location that was just out of sight because the lake curved and the trail merged into the trees.

"Where's the pup?" Tony asked.

Tilly barked once, then turned around and ran back the way she'd just come.

"We should follow her," I said.

We set off in the direction Tilly had run. When we rounded the corner and cleared the trees, we saw the pup standing at the edge of the water, looking at what seemed to be a man floating in the water.

"Oh God," I said, and Tony and I both waded in.

Chapter 3

Tony used his satellite phone to call 911 as soon as we realized we were much too late to help the man. We were told to wait with the body but not to disturb it. Of course, we were both soaking wet and it was freezing cold, so in the end we decided to call Mike and have him wait with the body while we went back to the cabin to change our clothes. By the time Mike had arrived to watch over the body and we'd walked the dogs back to the house, changed, and returned, the local police had shown up.

"Who is it?" I asked Mike.

"According to the officer who responded, the victim's name is Doug Peterman. He's a local who works as a maintenance man. He, along with his wife Gwen, clean and repair the cabins after each tenant moves out."

"How long has he been dead?" I asked.

"My best guess is a day or two," Mike answered.

"A day or two? Did his wife report him missing?"

"Apparently not. The police will follow up to see what she knows. The officer in charge has Conrad Bilson, the man who runs this place, on the phone right now. Let's wait to see if he wants to speak to the two of you. Then we can head back and let the local PD do their job."

Tony and I stayed with Mike while the officer finished his call. As soon as he hung up, he came over to us.

"Officer Holderman, this is my sister, Tess Thomas, and her boyfriend, Tony Marconi. They were walking their dogs when they came upon the body in the lake."

"I understand you're renting the retreat house," Officer Holderman began.

"If you mean the big house on the north end of the lake, yes," I answered. "My mother rented it. We just arrived maybe twenty minutes before we set off to walk the dogs."

"According to Conrad Bilson, he'd last seen Mr. Peterson when he picked up the key to the house on Friday afternoon to clean it and do some minor repairs after the group from Techucom left that morning."

"Techucom?" I asked.

"Bilson built the house on the north end of the lake to cater to groups, mainly corporations, looking for a place to hold corporate retreats. A tech company from California had rented the house for the past month. They just left, so, according to Bilson, he sent Peterson to get it ready for your arrival today. Did you happen to notice if there was any evidence of foul play when you arrived at the house?"

"No," I answered. "But I was only inside for a minute. I just went up to our room, checked on my cats, changed my shoes, and grabbed my jacket." I looked at Mike. He'd been in the house the longest of any of us.

"I had a good look around," Mike said. "The door was securely locked when we arrived. I poked my head into all the rooms when I was unloading the luggage with the exception of the door behind the kitchen, which was locked."

"That's the room a lot of the renters use as a conference or meeting room," Officer Holderman informed us. "It's mostly empty, with only a table and a monitor in it, so I'm not sure why it would be locked." Holderman looked toward his men, who had just finished bagging the body. "I'm going to check with the others for a few minutes, then I'll be going up to the house. The three of you are free to go. If I have any other questions, I'll ask them when I arrive."

"What about the wife?" I asked the officer. "Doesn't it seem odd that she didn't report her husband missing?"

"Bilson told me she's been visiting her sister for the past few weeks. She isn't due back until Tuesday. I'll call her once I wrap things up here."

I'd never even met Doug Peterman, but I found his death had jarred me. I supposed it was natural to be upset after finding a dead body. Still, there was nothing I could do to change things, and this trip was important to my mother for reasons I still didn't understand, so I vowed to do my best not to let the man's death put too much of a damper on my mood.

When we arrived at the house, the puppy ran over to Mike, wiggling and wagging his whole body. "Someone's happy to see you." I laughed.

Mike bent over and gave the pup a pat on the head. "There, there, good boy. Now shoo."

The pup totally ignored the shoo part, instead sitting on Mike's foot.

"I think you have a new buddy," Bree said.

"He's not my buddy; he's just a stray," Mike countered.

"Maybe we should name him," Mom said.

"He doesn't need a name," Mike insisted. "I'm sure we'll figure out where he belongs when we start asking around. Remind me to mention it to Holderman when he gets here."

"Holderman?" Mom asked.

"Officer Holderman." Mike walked over and stood in front of the fire Mom or Bree must have started while we were gone. "He's coming by in a while to take a look at the house."

"Why does he want to see the house?" Bree asked.

"It seems the last time the man was seen, at least the last time he was seen by Conrad Bilson, who owns this place, was Friday afternoon, when he stopped by the camp store to pick up the key. He was supposed to clean it and take care of a few minor repairs. He never returned the key, though Bilson did tell Officer Holderman that he wasn't expecting him to do that until Saturday."

"The place looks clean," Tony commented.

Mike nodded. "True. Which means that whatever happened to him happened after he finished up here."

"Are we safe in the house?" Mom asked.

"I'm sure we are," Mike replied.

"Do you know how the man died?" I asked.

"It appears he was shot in the back. I'm assuming that was the cause of death." Mike bent down and picked up the pup, who had been sitting on his foot the entire time we were talking. The pup wagged his tail and licked Mike's face. Mike smiled before setting him back on the floor. Oh yeah; that pup had found a new daddy if the old one wasn't located.

"Should I start dinner?" Mom asked when there was a brief lull in the conversation.

"I'd wait until after Holderman has his look around," Mike answered. "He should be here any minute."

As if on cue, there was a knock on the door.

"Come on in," Mike invited him inside. "This is my mother, Lucy Thomas, and my girlfriend, Bree Price. You've met Tess and Tony."

"I'm sorry for the inconvenience," Holderman said. "I'll try to be quick so you can get back to your holiday."

"Do you know what happened to that man?" Mom asked.

"Not yet, ma'am. How did you find the place when you arrived?"

"It was clean, if that's what you're asking," Mike answered. "If there was a group that left on Friday morning, I'd say Peterman cleaned the house and took care of any repairs before anything happened to him."

"You said the conference room was locked?" Holderman asked.

"Yes. I tried the handle just after we arrived and it was locked," Mike said. "I didn't think much about it.

I've rented houses before where the owner keeps a locked room for personal property."

"Do you mind if I take a look?" Holderman asked.

"Help yourself." Mike led the way to the room, although it was clear Holderman knew where it was.

He tried the knob, which confirmed the door was locked. He took a tool out of his pocket and picked the lock. He opened it and stepped inside. Mike followed him, and I followed Mike. The others waited in the hallway.

"It looks like someone's been in here," Holderman said as he looked around. "And he or she probably entered through the window."

I glanced at the window, which had been left open a crack. The screen had been removed and was on the ground outside. As Holderman indicated it would be, the room was empty, except for a long table surrounded by ten chairs and a computer monitor hanging on a wall.

"Would the key Peterman picked up have opened this room?" I asked.

Holderman frowned. "I'm not sure. I'll need to check with Bilson."

"A few things aren't lining up for me," I said. "The room is empty, as you said it would be, so why lock it? And for the room to be entered from the outside, the window would have had to have been unlocked and maybe even partially open to get a grip on it. Why would it be open even a crack? It's freezing."

"Tess is right," Mike said. "It's likely someone, probably Peterman, was working inside when someone arrived. Someone he was afraid of or wanted to avoid."

"So he locked himself in the conference room," I continued Mike's thought, "then opened the window and slipped out."

Officer Holderman bent over to take a look at the window lock. "That's not a bad theory, although I don't suppose it's the only one possible. If that's what happened, I'd say whoever Peterman was trying to avoid caught up with him."

We had the all-clear to go on with our evening and Holderman left. Tony, Mom, and Bree headed to the kitchen to get dinner ready, and Mike went outside to bring in more wood for the fire. And I went upstairs to check on the cats, who were still locked in the bedroom.

"Sorry, guys," I said as I entered the room. "It's been a little hectic, but I think it's okay to come out now."

I decided I'd move the food, water, and litter box down to the laundry room I'd seen off the kitchen. Hopefully, Mike's new puppy wouldn't harass the cats because I intended to set up the food and water for the dogs in the same room. Maybe I'd put the cats' food as well as their beds on top of the long counter I'd seen so they could escape the dogs if they chose to. I was fortunate in that neither Tang nor Tinder were afraid of or intimidated by dogs in general. They were used to being around Tilly and Titan, and I didn't think the pup would actually hurt them. He was interested in them for sure, but it seemed as if he just wanted to play.

After I got all the animals settled, I went upstairs with the dog beds we'd brought for Tilly and Titan. I was going to suggest to Mike that he let the pup sleep in his room, but if he wasn't willing to do that, I'd use the extra blankets I found in the hall closet to make up a bed near Tilly. In my mind I knew there was a good likelihood we'd find the pup's owner, but based on the interaction between Mike and him, I had a gut feeling the two were meant to be together, even though neither Mike nor Bree had ever shown any interest in having a dog.

By the time I made it back down to join the others, the kitchen elves had something wonderful smelling in the oven and Mike had a roaring fire crackling away in the fireplace.

"What smells so good?" I asked.

"It's a baked ziti Tony threw together while I made us cheesecake for dessert and Bree made salad and sliced the rosemary bread," Mom said.

I could see I was going to have to do a lot of hiking on this trip if I wanted my jeans to fit as well at the end of it as they did today.

"Wine?" Mike asked, holding up a bottle.

"Please." I accepted a glass. "I have Tony's and my animals all settled, but we'll need to use blankets to make up a bed for the pup." I looked at him. "I thought we could put him in your room." I glanced down at the puppy, who was sitting at his feet. "He seems quite taken with you."

Mike hesitated, and surprisingly, it was Bree who spoke up. "Yes, let's put him in our room. You already have enough animals to trip over."

"Okay," I said. "I'll make up something after dinner."

"I think we need to give the little guy a name," Mom repeated.

"We aren't keeping him," Mike countered. "He's just here until we find his owner."

"Still," Mom volleyed. "I think he should at least have a temporary name while he's with us."

"How about Scamp?" Bree said.

"Or Baxter," I suggested.

"I've always been fond of Coop," Tony said.

"His name will be Leonard," Mike asserted.

I lifted a brow. "Leonard? Why Leonard?"

"Why not? It's a name. And Mom says he needs one."

I glanced at Bree, who just shrugged. "Okay," I said. "Leonard it is."

I supposed Leonard liked his new name just fine based on the look of adoration he continued to send up at Mike.

"Let's just fill our plates buffet style, then take them to the dining table," Mom suggested.

We agreed as Tony took the ziti out of the oven and Bree slid the bread in to heat. Mom set out plates while I grabbed the salad and Mike topped off everyone's wine. I was having the best time. I just hoped the rest of the week would go as smoothly as tonight. Of course, I supposed if you took the death of a local man into account, today might not have gone as smoothly as it could have.

After dinner, Tony and Mike did the dishes, Mom went into her room to unpack, and Bree and I headed upstairs to make up a bed for the pup.

"Leonard sure is in love with Mike," I said.

Bree paused. "Yeah. He really is. And I can tell Mike is a little in love with him. We need to get out tomorrow and really try to find the pup's owner. If he has one, it will be best to get him back to his person before Mike becomes too attached. If we don't find the owner, though, this week will be a good time for Mike and Leonard to bond."

"So you're okay with the dog?"

Bree looked surprised. "Sure. Why wouldn't I be?"

"Your house is just so... white."

Bree laughed. "Granted, when I decorated, a puppy with muddy feet wasn't part of the plan, but Tilly's always been welcome, and if Mike adopts Leonard, I'll welcome him as well."

"Yeah, but Tilly is neat and lies quietly in her bed when she comes to visit. Leonard is a puppy. He's bound to get into something at some point."

Bree shrugged. "So I'll replace the white carpet with hardwood and trade my white sofa in for something made of leather. It'll be fine."

I smiled. Bree had no idea how happy I was to hear her say that.

Once the dishes were done and Leonard's bed was made up from the blankets I'd found in the linen closet, Tony and I bundled up and took the three dogs out for a walk before we all retired to our own rooms for the evening. The dogs seemed to have a lot of pent-up energy for some reason, so we took them on an extralong walk despite the layer of fresh snow that had fallen while we were eating. I'd checked the local forecast earlier, and it appeared the next day or two would see mostly flurries, but the possibility of a heavy snow increased dramatically as the week went on. It would be fun to sit in the cozy house and watch it snow. The main living area featured a wall of windows that overlooked the lake, which would make a winter storm even more beautiful to watch. I could imagine curling up by the fire with a mug of hot cocoa as huge flakes drifted slowly from the dark sky.

"Did you see where Leonard went?" Tony asked, his voice breaking into my daydream.

I paused to look around. "There," I pointed. "He just darted around the side of the house. It seemed like he was chasing something. Hopefully, a squirrel or a rabbit and not a raccoon or a skunk." I took a step toward the spot where I'd last seen the pup. "I'll get him."

I headed around to the side of the house but didn't see the pup right away, so I took out my phone and turned on the flashlight app. "Leonard," I called.

The pup, who'd crawled into the crawl space under the house, let out a bark. I hurried over to get him just as I noticed the puppy's footprints weren't the only ones in the snow. "Tony," I called.

He hurried over to where I'd bent down for a closer look.

"What is it?" he asked.

"Footprints."

Tony jogged forward until he was beside me. "Fresh footprints."

I stood up. "These were left after it snowed." They trailed from the forest to the kitchen window and then back to the forest again. "Someone was watching us."

"Yeah," Tony groaned. "We'd better tell Mike."

Chapter 4

Monday, November 19

Mike had called Officer Holderman, who'd instructed Mike to take photos of the prints and lock up tight before going to bed. He pointed out that several of the other cabins had tenants, and the prints could have been made by someone out for a walk who'd gotten curious and wandered over to the house for a peek. I supposed he could be right. Footprints in the snow didn't necessarily mean anything. We probably wouldn't have given them a second thought if we hadn't found a body in the lake just hours earlier. Holderman advised us to keep our eyes and ears open but not to worry too much unless something happened that led us to believe the footprints belonged to more than just a curious hiker.

Mike was intent on finding Leonard's owner today, so the four of us split up and each took a side of the lake. We'd knock on doors and ask around. Mom was happy to stay in the nice, warm house with the cats while she baked a cake. Tony and I took Tilly and Titan and started out along the eastern shore, while Mike and Bree took Leonard and went west.

It was overcast today, with a few flurries in the air from time to time, but so far any sort of serious storm had held off. I dressed in my heavy jeans, sturdy boots, wool sweater, and bright red down jacket. Tony and I held hands and chatted about the upcoming holiday as we made our way along the road to the first cabin on our side of the lake.

"It looks empty," I said when we arrived at the smallish log cabin a few feet from the lake.

"Yeah. There aren't any tire tracks in the snow. When we drove around to the house yesterday, I noticed most of the cabins appeared vacant. I wonder if they're all rentals or if some have permanent residents."

"That would be a good question for Conrad Bilson. The little store is closed today, but I wonder if he'd mind if we stopped by his house. I'm assuming the large cabin near the little settlement as you arrive is his personal lodging."

"I guess it wouldn't hurt to knock on the door when we get around to that part of the lake." Tony turned away from the empty cabin and continued down the road. "Was it around this time of the fall when your dad visited every year?"

It had been so long, it was hard to remember. "I think it might have been earlier in the month. I remember him being home for Halloween. He'd sit in his chair trying to watch TV while my mom handled the trick-or-treaters. He'd grumble about all the interruptions, even yelled at Mom to turn off the porch light and pull the blinds. Mom would argue it was Halloween, and trick-or-treating was a lovely tradition that should be embraced rather than avoided. Dad would get mad enough to head out to the bar and Mom would hand out candy until it was gone."

"Sounds stressful."

I shrugged. "Oh, I don't know. Dad grumbling and storming off to the bar and Mom upholding traditions despite his orneriness was sort of one of our traditions. I very clearly remember that first Halloween after Dad died. I was too old to go out trick-or-treating and Mom thought I was too young to go to the party Mike was going to attend. I stayed home with Mom and handed out candy. I kept glancing at Dad's chair the whole evening and really missing his grumbling and complaining about the dag-nab kids interrupting whatever boring show he'd been watching."

Tony squeezed my hand. "I guess your memories are your memories, and you miss what you had when it's gone."

"Exactly. I also remember Dad being home for Thanksgiving. I think he came up to the lake between the two holidays. Mom would remember more specifically, I'm sure, but I do know he'd always miss my school play, which was held the week before Thanksgiving. What I don't remember is if he missed it because he was working or fishing."

"I guess he must have missed a lot of stuff when you were a kid."

I nodded. "Most of it, actually. Mom was great. She was there a hundred percent, never missed a single play, concert, or sporting event. Dad was always away, but it was always that way, so I don't think I was too upset that he missed so much."

"I'm not going to miss a single thing," Tony said as we neared the second cabin. "When I have kids, I'm going to be present in their everyday lives."

I smiled. "Yeah. Me too." I looked at the cabin, which didn't have a car in the drive but did have smoke coming from the chimney. "Should we knock on the door?"

"Let's." Tony started forward.

After instructing the dogs to wait and climbing the three steps, which hadn't been shoveled, we knocked on the hardwood door. After a minute, an older man with a mop of white hair answered. "Help you?"

"My name is Tony, and this is Tess," Tony began. "We're staying in the big house at the end of the lake and we found a puppy." Tony held out his phone, which had a photo of Leonard on it. "We're hoping to find his owner. I don't suppose you know who he belongs to?"

The man looked at the photo. "Nope. Never seen this dog before."

"Are you a renter or a long-term resident?" I asked.

"I'm here for the winter. Been coming to this cabin every winter for more than twenty years. Too crowded in the summer, so I head north then."

I tried to appear casually interested. "Really? My dad used to come up here every year. He liked to fish. I don't suppose you remember him—Grant Thomas?"

He shook his head. "No. The name doesn't ring a bell."

I pulled up a photo of him that I'd scanned into my phone, standing next to Mike, that was taken the year before he'd died. "Maybe this will jar your memory."

He looked at it. "You talking about Tuck?"

"Tuck?" I asked.

"The man standing next to the young man. He came up here every year around this time to spend time with Finn."

"Finn?" I asked. "Does he live in this area?"

"He did. Died about fourteen or fifteen years ago, I guess. He was standing at the edge of the lake, fishing and minding his own business, when he was shot clean through the head. Never did find out who did it. Some say he was hit by a stray bullet from one of the hunters in the area, others that he was killed by a sniper." The man frowned. "You know, it seems like Tuck might have been with him when he was shot. Been a while and my memory isn't what it used to be, but I know someone was with Finn and called it in. I guess Conrad might remember. He recalls things better than me."

I glanced at Tony. I couldn't help but notice the serious expression on his face.

"Do you remember if Tuck continued to come to the lake after Finn died?" I asked.

He shook his head. "I don't recall seeing him again after that. Guess his primary reason for coming was to spend time with Finn, so it made sense that he didn't come around again after he died."

Well, that answered one of my questions. I'd been hoping my dad continued to come, and if he did, maybe someone around here would know how to contact him.

"Do things like that happen often up here?" Tony asked.

"Things like what?" he asked.

"Unexplained deaths. I guess you heard about Doug Peterman."

The man narrowed his gaze. "What happened to Doug Peterman?"

"His body was found floating in the lake," Tony said.

The man's eyes grew two sizes. "Doug's dead?"

Tony bowed his head. "I'm afraid so."

The man's expression shuttered. "Sorry to hear that, but I have grits on the stove I should get back to. You take care now." He closed the door, and based on the very distinct sound of a rod being pushed into place, locked it.

"What do you make of that?" I asked.

Tony took my hand and led me down the steps. "He knows something he isn't comfortable sharing. Of course, we're complete strangers. Maybe Holderman can get the rest of the story."

The next three cabins were empty, and the fourth was occupied by a young couple, who, like us, was here for the holiday. They hadn't seen the puppy before and had only been to the lake one time before now and didn't know either my dad or Doug Peterman. The fifth cabin was being used by four men for a guys' retreat. They hadn't been around back when my dad used to come here, and none admitted to have ever seen the puppy, but they knew Peterman and, while they had no idea who might have wanted to hurt him, they were sorry to hear he was dead.

"Just a few more," I said to Tony.

"There's a truck parked at the cabin up ahead."

Judging from the distance to the southern end of the lake, I estimated there were only two or three more cabins on this side before we'd come to the end at the little village. I just hoped someone was staying in one of those cabins who could provide additional information about the puppy or Finn and Tuck.

As we had before, we told the dogs to stay, climbed the steps, and knocked on the door. A middle-aged man with short brown hair answered. We introduced ourselves, and he told us his name was Tom Flanders.

"How can I help you?" he asked.

We started off with a question about the dog, who he had not seen. I then asked him if he was a vacationer or a long-term renter. He'd moved in two years ago and lived in the cabin year-round. We asked him if he'd heard about Peterman, and he had. I asked if we could come in to speak with him for a minute, and he stepped aside. I told the dogs to stay, and Tony and I followed him inside.

His cabin was larger and in much better condition than the others we'd visited today. It was obvious it was a home, not just a place to vacation. There was art on the walls, a huge telescope looking out over the lake, and photos of a woman with dark hair and an inviting smile lined up on one of the built-in bookshelves.

"How exactly can I help you?" he asked.

He didn't ask us to sit down, which seemed to indicate he preferred we ask our questions quickly and leave. "I'm not sure what you've heard, but Mr. Peterman was shot in the back before he ended up in the lake. Given that he was killed here, I suspect someone at the lake was the one who kill him. Any idea who might want him dead?" I asked.

Flanders frowned. "I think you might be wrong about someone from here being the one to kill him. At least not any of the long-term renters. You never know about the people who spend a weekend or even a few weeks on the lake. What I do know is that Doug was a good guy. Well-liked by all the locals. His wife too."

"Do you remember the last time you saw him?"

His gaze narrowed. "Is there a reason you're asking all these questions?"

I tilted my head toward Tony. "We were the ones who found the body. I guess we're just curious about how he ended up in the water. From what I understand, he was at the big house on the other end of the lake on Friday afternoon. We're staying there now."

"I hadn't spoken to Doug in almost a week, but I saw his truck parked at the retreat house at around ten o'clock on Friday evening. If I were you, I'd be looking for clues in that house. I don't know offhand who would want to hurt him, but I can tell you there's been something odd going on since those science folks showed up."

"Science folks?" I asked.

"Some big tech firm leased the place for an entire month. During that time, there were groups coming and going. I'm not sure what they were doing, but they sure weren't here to enjoy the mountains or the lake. Mostly they'd stay up real late at night. I could see the lights and folks walking around inside from my place if I looked directly across the lake."

I glanced at the telescope, which was positioned perfectly to do just that.

"And then there were the trucks," he added.

"Trucks?" Tony asked.

"Panel trucks. Couldn't see what was inside them. They weren't marked in any way, so they could just be bringing supplies, but the whole thing seemed odd. Why come all the way out here for a meeting if you aren't ever going to leave the house during the day? Seems it would be easier to just meet somewhere close to an airport."

Flanders had a point. It did seem that Lake Timberland was a long way from anything to come for a corporate retreat if you were going to stay inside and conduct meetings all day.

He continued. "Doug mentioned he'd been seeing some odd stuff when he went in to clean. He wouldn't say what, but I'm going to go out on a limb and say that it was whatever he saw that got him killed."

"So Peterman went in to clean during the month the house was leased by Techucom?" I verified.

"Once a week. It's part of the least agreement."

"Did you tell Officer Holderman that?" Tony asked.

"Yeah, I told him. He said he'd look into it. Guess he will."

Suddenly, I wondered if staying in the house was the best idea. Was whatever had been going on a thing of the past or something we might need to be aware of?

After a few more minutes, we thanked Flanders and continued on our way. There were three other empty cabins before we wound up at the house I assumed belonged to Conrad Bilson. We knocked on the door, but there wasn't an answer, and the little store and laundromat were closed, so we turned around and headed back the way we'd come.

"Something on your mind?" Tony asked after we'd walked in silence for a while.

"A lot of things," I said. "I'm wondering what Peterman might have seen that could have gotten him killed, and if staying at the house might be putting us in some sort of danger. Have you ever heard of Techucom?"

"Sure. They're a multibillion-dollar corporation. I can't tell you exactly what they're currently developing, but I know they do a lot of stealthy communications stuff.

"Stealthy communications?"

"Experimental stuff. They have several government contracts. I imagine they're probably heavily involved in projects for the military."

"Does it seem odd to you that a huge corporation with government contracts would hold their retreats all the way up here?"

"Not necessarily. It's pretty private up here, if they were planning on testing."

"I guess that's true. I'm curious about the panel trucks and what they might have been hauling. I wonder if they were working on some sort of top-secret military operation."

"It's possible. However, if you're thinking Peterman stumbled onto some sort of highly classified government secret and was killed to keep him quiet, I doubt it."

I shrugged. "I'm sure you're right. And while I'm interested to find out who shot Doug Peterman and why, I'm more interested in finding out who Finn was, who shot him, how he was related to my dad, and why my dad was calling himself Tuck when he was here."

"We can ask Bilson about Finn. The store should be open tomorrow."

"We can. And I can ask my mom if she remembers someone named Finn."

"And how are you going to work that into the conversation?" Tony asked.

"I'll just say we ran into someone who remembered Dad when we were looking for the dog's owner, spending time with someone named Finn. I don't need to mention that Dad went by an alias, or that we were intentionally digging for the information."

"I guess it's plausible the information about Finn could have come up during casual conversation. Especially if you introduced yourself and the man remembered the surname, although Thomas isn't uncommon."

"I doubt Mom will ask for details. If she does, I'll just say I mentioned that Dad used to come to the lake and the man remembered him. I wonder what Mom plans to make for dinner."

"Are you really hungry after that huge breakfast we had?"

"Breakfast was hours ago, and this mountain air is making me hungry. I know she brought a roast. It's been a while since I've had one of Mom's slow-cooked roasts with baby carrots and red potatoes."

"That does sound good," Tony agreed. "But it's only two o'clock. I think maybe we might want to grab a snack to tide us over."

"Mom brought some cheese and crackers. I think there might be cold cuts too. My feet are freezing despite my wool socks. Settling in by the fire with a glass of wine and a cheese tray sounds pretty darn relaxing."

Tony leaned over and kissed my neck. "There are other ways to warm up your feet."

I hit his shoulder. "Not in the middle of the day with my mom right there in the kitchen. But later. Definitely."

Chapter 5

As I hoped, when we returned to the house, Mom confirmed she was making pot roast with all the trimmings for dinner. Mike and Bree hadn't returned yet, but when I mentioned I was going to make a snack, Mom helped me put together a cheese and deli tray that we took into the living room, where Tony had stoked up the fire. The three of us shared a bottle of his expensive wine while we nibbled on our snack. Mom shared ideas for the week ahead while Tony and I gave her an abbreviated version of our search for Leonard's owner. After a bit, Tony went out to chop some more wood, so it was just Mom and me.

"It's so sad that little pup is on his own," Mom said. "But it looks like Mike might step up if the owner isn't found."

"I had the same thought, By the way, we ran into a long-term renter who remembered Dad."

Mom raised a brow. "Really?"

"He said Dad came here to visit someone named Finn. I tried to think back, but I'm sure I don't remember anyone named Finn."

Mom shook her head. "Your father never mentioned a Finn. He used to tell me he was coming up to the lake to spend some alone time. I never really bought it. If I'm completely honest, I suspected he was having an affair."

I frowned. "If you thought he was having an affair, why didn't you confront him?"

Mom shrugged. "It wouldn't have made a difference. I do feel a sense of relief in the idea that he was here to visit a friend, not a lover."

This was a very odd conversation to be having with my mother. I'd confirmed she hadn't known Finn, so I changed the subject. "Did Dad go on other trips?"

Mom laughed, an empty, hollow sort of laugh. "Dad seemed to be going one place or another most of the time. He wasn't around all that much."

"Did he talk about his trips with you at all?"

Mom shook her head. "No. Never."

"And you were okay with that?"

"In the beginning it bothered me that I didn't know a thing about his life outside the time he spent in White Eagle, but as time went on, I learned to accept the way things were. If I had it to do all over again, I might behave differently, but I have you and Mike, so I don't regret the decisions I made."

It occurred to me that it was very odd indeed that a man's wife wouldn't know about his life outside the context of the time they shared. Had it always been that way? I tried to think back. I had never met any of my relatives on Dad's side of the family. I suppose as a child I wondered about grandparents and cousins, but I had my mom's parents, siblings, and nieces and nephews to call family, so I didn't agonize too much over it. Still, from where I sat now, it was odd. "You know, I was thinking about family when I was working with Aunt Ruthie on the family tree I've been playing around with, and I realized not only did I never meet Dad's parents, but I don't even know their names or where they lived. I know Dad didn't like to talk about them. I assume they were estranged before I was even born. But I do find I'm curious."

Mom averted my eyes as she answered. "I'm sorry. I never met them either. And I'm afraid I don't know their names, or even where they lived."

"You never asked Dad about them?"

Mom glanced at me. "Oh, I asked. More than once. In the beginning. I thought it odd that Grant was so unwilling to give me even a clue about his past. I figured he just needed time to come around to telling me whatever it was he was going out of his way not to, but as time went on, I realized your father's life before he arrived in White Eagle was totally off the table. I didn't like it. As you know, family is important to me. But it was made clear to me that the matter wasn't open for discussion, and if I couldn't accept that, he'd move on. I chose to accept it."

I let out a breath. "Wow. I'm not sure I could live with that degree of ambiguity."

Mom's expression softened. "You live with what you're forced to live with."

I sat back and let what she'd said bounce around in my mind. Tony had said Grant Thomas didn't seem to exist until shortly before he met and married my mom. We had several theories about why that might have been, but the knowledge that even Mom didn't know where he'd come from was surprising.

"So Dad never told you where he grew up or anything at all about his past?" I knew I should let it go, but I found I couldn't.

"No. As I said, his past was off the table."

I put my hand on Mom's. "I'm sorry. That must have been hard."

She put her other hand on top of mine. "It was hard, but it was the deal I made."

"Do you ever regret that decision?"

Mom leaned back into the softness of the sofa. "There were times, when your dad was still alive, when I wondered how my life would have turned out if I had chosen differently. But then I'd look at you and Mike and know that if I had to do it over again, I would do exactly the same thing." She paused before going on. "You're probably picking up on the fact that your dad and I didn't have the perfect marriage. I never wanted you or Mike to know about the struggles we had. Grant was a good man. He worked hard and took care of his family. And he loved you both. Very much. I hope I haven't said anything that will cause you to doubt that."

"No," I assured Mom. "Nothing you've said has changed my opinion about Dad. If anything, I feel like I have a better understanding of things. I'll admit to having a few unanswered questions now that I'm older and beginning to put pieces of my moments with Dad together. I'm curious: If your marriage wasn't exactly happy, out of all the lakes in this area, why did you want to spend our vacation here?"

Mom lowered her eyes. "I guess I have a few unanswered questions of my own. I thought perhaps I'd find them here."

"About what?" I asked.

Mom stood up. "It's not important. I think I've said enough for one day. I need to check my roast, and then I think I'll lay down for a bit. We should eat around six thirty."

I could feel the tension build in my shoulders as she walked out of the room. I wondered what that was all about. I'd give Mom her space now, but before the week was over, I fully intended to find out more about what she was struggling with.

Tony came in with an armload full of wood just as Mom headed into the kitchen. I filled him in briefly on our conversation while he placed new logs on the low embers. We agreed that while we wanted answers, the last thing we wanted to do was to cause Mom any sadness or discomfort, though that seemed to be what we were doing by digging around in Dad's past.

We sat down on the sofa, and I put my head on his shoulder and thought back to the conversation I'd had with her a month ago, after Tony found the photo of her standing on the same bridge Jared Collins had been. I hadn't talked with her all that much about Dad before then. She'd revealed her love affair with Collins, and admitted she never loved Dad the way she had this other unobtainable man. She'd told me about her trip to Europe, her heartbreak, and her decision to enter into a relationship with a man she met back in the States who looked a whole lot like him. While they looked almost like twins, they were very different people. Collins was open and loving, while my dad was distant and withdrawn.

Tony and I hadn't figured out why Collins was being investigated by Senator Kline, and after we realized he and my dad weren't the same person, we'd stopped trying. We'd decided to focus our energy on finding my dad, though now I wondered if we might have given up our research into Jared Collins a little too early.

I was about to bring that up when Mike and Bree walked in. "Any luck?" I asked.

"No one admits ever having seen the dog, and we confirmed with them that there aren't any houses where we found him," Bree said.

I looked at Mike and smiled. "Congratulations. It looks like you just became a dad."

I was expecting a flat-out refusal, but instead he shrugged and helped himself to some cheese.

"We got some information about Doug Peterman," she said.

"We did too," I replied. "What did you find?"

"We talked to a man named Harris Beaufort, who said he'd run into Peterman at the bar in the next little town over at around eight on Friday evening. Peterman mentioned he'd been at the lake, cleaning one of the houses, but he was finished and planned to take the rest of the weekend off."

"A man we spoke to today said he saw Peterman's truck in front of the house at around ten p.m. I guess he might have left and then come back for some reason."

Bree lifted a shoulder. "I guess."

"Anything else?" I asked.

"We saw a man pulled onto the side of the road. He was driving a black truck with tinted windows, and it was sitting in an odd spot. I had Bree wait with Leonard and went over to talk to him. I asked if he'd broken down, but he said he hadn't, that he was waiting for someone, though he didn't say who. Bree and I drove on, but the man we spoke to at the next house commented that he'd seen a man in a black truck lingering in the area. I don't know if it means anything, but I plan to call Holderman to fill him in."

Tony and I went to freshen up before dinner and Bree did the same, while Mike made his call. I didn't have a grasp on what was going on with Peterman's death at this point, but my gut told me that just because we were visitors who'd never met him didn't mean we'd be off the hook for any fallout from whatever was going on.

******

Dinner was amazing. Afterward, Tony and I volunteered to take on cleanup duties, while Mike and Bree took the three dogs for a walk and Mom said good night and retired to her suite. It was only a little past eight, so I was somewhat concerned that she was turning in so early. She'd been quiet during dinner, and I suspected she might still have our conversation from earlier on her mind.

When Tony and I finished in the kitchen and Mike and Bree returned with the dogs, the four of us headed outside to take a soak in the hot tub. It was a clear, starry night despite the overcast skies earlier in the day, and the zillions of stars overhead were like a tapestry that had been arranged just for our enjoyment.

"Now this is the life," I said as I melted into the hot water. The stress I had been holding on to seemed to evaporate with the steam that rose into the frigid air.

"I've been thinking about getting a hot tub for my place," Mike said. "Of course, it would only be one more thing to dig out every time it snows."

"You could build a cover over it, but then you wouldn't be able to look up at the stars," I said.

"There was a hot tub at the little house I rented before I bought my house," Bree reminded me. "The concept was nice, but I never really used it. It isn't as if I was on vacation and had a lot of free time. When I thought to use it, it was usually on a cold winter night, and as Mike said, the need to dig it out before I could use it had me settling for a glass of wine or a cup of tea in front of the fire."

"A fire sounds good, but I'm not sure it would melt away my stress the way this hot tub does," I countered.

"It's too bad Mom is missing out," Mike said. "She looked sort of stressed at dinner. Did something happen I don't know about?"

I didn't answer immediately. I hadn't shared any of the information Tony and I had dug up about my dad with Mike yet, but I assumed at some point I would. I wasn't certain this was the best time to do it. Still, he deserved the truth. "Mom and I got onto a conversation about Dad. I'm not sure if I told you, but Aunt Ruthie has been helping me build a family tree, and while I'm making good progress on Mom's side of the family, I haven't found a single thing on Dad's."

"I guess he never really talked about his relatives," Mike said.

"Not at all. I didn't even have names to plug into the spots for paternal grandparents, so I asked Mom about them, and it turns out she doesn't know either."

Mike frowned. "She doesn't know the names of Dad's parents?"

"No, she doesn't," I confirmed. "She asked about his family and his past when they met, and he said all that was off the table. She didn't push, but as time went by and she could see he was never going to volunteer any information, she asked again, and he basically told her the door to his past was closed and if she couldn't accept that, he'd move on. She chose to accept it."

Mike sat up a bit. "You know, as a kid I used to wonder. I asked Dad a few times about our grandparents, and he just said they were dead. I thought it was strange that no one from Dad's family came around or sent cards or gifts or anything, but that's the way it is in some families, and I don't suppose it bothered me all that much. I do remember wondering why we still hadn't heard from anyone when he died. I figured his parents were dead and he might not have siblings, so maybe there really wasn't anyone, but in the back of my mind I felt there was more to it."

"Now that your dad is gone, he can't get mad if you have Tony poke around a bit," Bree suggested. "He should at least be able to find a birth certificate that will give you his parents' names for your family tree."

I glanced at Tony. He shrugged, and I decided to respond. "I didn't tell Mom this part because I could see she was getting upset, but I already had Tony do that."

"And...?" Mike asked.

"And according to what Tony could find, Grant Thomas didn't exist before 1981."

Mike sat forward. "What do you mean, he didn't exist?"

"He couldn't find any school, work, or financial records for Grant Walton Thomas," I said. "Tony couldn't find a birth certificate, a driver's license, or a passport, nothing."

"There has to be a mistake. That's impossible. Of course he existed," Mike spat out. "Tony must have missed something."

"He didn't miss anything. In fact, he spent a lot of time on it," I said. Mike was getting angry and agitated, and I hated that this conversation was ruining our evening, but I supposed there never was going to be a good time to talk about this. Now that I'd started, I figured I may as well go all-in. "I didn't want to bring it up until I knew more, but Tony and I have been looking in to it for a while."

"What exactly have you been looking in to?"

"Mike honey," Bree said, "why don't we let Tess tell us without jumping down her throat? I'm sure whatever she has to say is as difficult for her to talk about as it is for you to hear."

Mike took several deep breaths, then ran his hands over his face. He leaned back, then sat forward again. Eventually, he said, "I'm sorry, Tess. Please continue."

Tony took my hand in his beneath the water and gave it a little squeeze. I knew he'd been ready to jump in if needed, but this was my story to tell.

"Maybe we should get out of here and go inside," I began. "This is going to be a long story, and I'm not sure you're supposed to sit in water this warm for hours and hours."

Mike didn't answer.

"Let's meet in our room," I added. "I don't want Mom to overhear what I have to say, so we shouldn't talk in the living room. When you've heard it all, we can decide together what, if anything, to tell her."

"I think that's a good idea," Bree said, standing up, stepping over the edge of the hot tub, and grabbing a towel. "We'll get dressed and then we'll calmly talk this out." She looked at Mike and held out a hand. "Okay?"

Mike took her hand and stood up. "Okay."

To say I was nervous about how this talk would go was putting it mildly, but it was time to bring Mike into the loop, and being here seemed to offer the appropriate opportunity.

After we'd all gotten dressed, Bree and Mike came into Tony and my bedroom. We sat on the bed and they sat on the chairs that framed the fireplace.

"Before we begin, I want you to know that I was never intentionally keeping things from you. I suspected something and asked Tony to help me dig around, but I didn't want to bring anything up until I was certain, which I suppose I'm still not."

"It's fine, hon," Bree encouraged. "Just tell us."

I took a deep breath, blew it out slowly, and started to speak. "After Dad died and I'd had a chance to get over the shock of it, I began to think about things. I'm not sure why exactly, but thing just didn't seem to add up."

"What sort of things?" Mike asked.

"I just thought it was strange Dad died in this horrific crash, yet there was never any explanation about what happened. Was another car involved? Did he run into a ditch? Did he fall asleep at the wheel? Had he been drinking? And then there was the fact that there was no body. I get that he was badly burned, but all Mom received was an urn filled with ashes. She never even went to the town where the accident happened to view the body or verify that it was really Dad who died."

"There probably wasn't much left to see, and I'm sure Mom didn't want to leave us alone while she went to take a look," Mike said.

"Maybe. And maybe my questions just stemmed from an inability to accept what had happened. In those early days, I kept telling myself that maybe it was someone else who'd died in the crash and Dad was just fine. I even convinced myself the accident hadn't occurred at all, that it was just some big cover-up."

"You always did have an active imagination," Bree said.

"That's true. I did have a way of rewriting things in my head. The important thing, though, is that I was so sure something wasn't right that I asked Tony to help me find the truth."

"You weren't even friends back then," Bree pointed out.

"We weren't. But once we started working together, we became friends."

"So, did you find anything?" Mike asked.

"Not at first. In fact, not for twelve years. Then, last Christmas, Tony found this." I handed Mike the photo of Dad in front of the building in Los Angeles. Tony had printed all the photos we'd come across and brought them with us in case we needed them.

"That's Dad," Mike said.

"Yes, it is. When Tony found this photo, Dad had been dead for thirteen years," I said. "The building in the background was built ten years ago."

Mike went pale. He clutched the photo. "What are you saying? That Dad is alive?"

"We still don't know for sure," I answered. "Despite Tony's facial recognition software, which tagged the photo, we have no way to know for certain whether the man in the photo was Dad or someone who just looks an awful lot like him. You know, they say we all have a double. I didn't want to cause a fuss if it wasn't him, so I decided not to say anything until we knew more."

"And do you?" Mike asked. "Do you know more?"

"Yes, but let me get to it in a logical manner. It'll make more sense that way. Or at least as much sense as these very confusing things can."

"Okay. I'm sorry," Mike said. "Go ahead."

I looked at Tony. He gave me a look of encouragement. "While it had taken Tony twelve years to find this first photo, it only took another two months to find the next photo." I handed Mike the next one, of the interior of a convenience store. Behind the counter was a tall, skinny man with long, dark hair, a woman with a child of around five or six paying for a carton of milk and a box of doughnuts, and an older man standing off to the side. The latter, who looked like my father, was out of the line of vision of the camera but clearly visible in the security mirror. "This photo was taken in a minimart just outside Gallup, New Mexico. Tony already checked with the store, and no one there knew Dad. The store is attached to a truck stop, so we assume he was passing through."

"When was that one taken?" Mike asked.

"Two years ago."

Mike lost the little color he had in his face. "Two years ago?"

I nodded. "The frustrating thing about these photos is that they aren't traceable."

"What do you mean?" Bree asked.

Tony answered. "The photos I find with my software can be traced back to an origination point. Some were initially posted on social media, or maybe they appeared with a newspaper article. Other photos come from security or traffic cameras, or are associated with driver's licenses or some other form of identification. When I tried to run a trace on those two, I got nothing. Obviously, someone took the photos and uploaded them to a site accessible via the internet, but the source has been masked. I think we're looking at some extremely high-level security."

"So you're thinking Dad is involved in the government in some way?" Mike said.

"Maybe," I said. "We don't have all the pieces yet, but we do have something else."

"Go on," Mike said.

I considered telling him about Mom's connection with Jared Collins but decided against it. He was so protective of Mom, and me too, for that matter. "We didn't get any additional hits until last month. Then

Tony's facial recognition software tagged a photo that appeared to have been in real time."

"Real time?" Mike asked. "You mean it tagged a photo that was taken just minutes before you found out about it?"

Tony spoke. "It appeared that way. The photo seemed to have been taken somewhere in Eastern Europe, and as if the man was boarding a plane."

"What are you not saying?" Mike asked.

"The facial recognition program isn't infallible. It initially tagged a photo of someone named Jared Collins as being a match for your dad."

"Do you have this photo?" Mike asked.

I handed it to him.

Mike narrowed his gaze as he stared at the image. "This does look like it could be him." He looked up. "Have you had any other hits since then?"

"No," Tony answered. "Which isn't surprising. It's more surprising to me that we've gotten so many hits after years without any."

Bree ran her hands through her hair. "This sounds like the plot for a movie."

I glanced at Mike. "That's most of it. The only other thing we know we found out today. We showed Dad's photo to a man who winters here every year, and he recognized him. He knew Dad as Tuck, and he said he came to the lake to visit someone named Finn every year."

"Then we need to talk to this Finn," Mike said.

"He's dead. He was shot in the head fourteen or fifteen years ago while standing on the shore next to Dad. Apparently, they never figured out who shot him, and the man never saw Dad again."

Mike closed his eyes and leaned his head on the back of his chair. He looked shell-shocked, which was to be expected. I'd unloaded a lot on him all at once. It was going to take him time to process everything. I tried to imagine how totally overwhelming it would be if I'd found everything out in one huge lump. I'd had time to try to deal with the uncertainty of it all. Mike would need that as well. "I know you need time to think this over. We'll talk more tomorrow. But Mike," I said in a stern tone to get his attention, "don't say anything about all of this to Mom. She's already upset about what we talked about this afternoon. The last thing I want to do is ruin her whole vacation. Our spending time together as a family is very important to her."

Mike opened his eyes and sat up. "I won't say anything. Maybe the four of us can go for a walk tomorrow to go over things again. I'm sure once this sinks in, I'll have questions."

"That would be fine." I said. I got up and crossed the room, then put my arms around Mike and hugged him. "I'm sorry I didn't tell you sooner, but I'm very glad you know now."

I felt the tension leave my body as Mike hugged me back. It would take a while for him to wrap his head around everything, but I knew the two of us were going to be okay.

Chapter 6

Tuesday, November 20

After everything we'd talked about last night, I figured that would be the most stressful thing I'd need to deal with that week. I was wrong.

The next day started out okay. Mom, who was smiling and looked a lot better, had made everyone a spectacular breakfast. A storm had rolled in, so Tony and I had taken a quick and snowy walk with the dogs earlier while Mike built a fire, and Mom and Bree got food on the table. Mom's quiche was delicious and her homemade biscuits totally melted in your mouth. Last night, we'd talked about taking a hike today, but with the storm, it looked like our plans would have to be adjusted to board games by the fire. I really wasn't much of a board game sort of person, preferring the action of video games, but somehow, with the storm and the family together, they felt right. I should have known things wouldn't turn out as we'd planned;

things rarely did. We were just finishing up our meal when there was a knock on the door. Mike got up to answer it. When I saw that our morning caller was Officer Holderman, and that he wanted to speak to Mike in private, I knew our lazy day in front of the fire was going to be discarded completely.

"Is everything okay?" Mom asked after Holderman left.

"The officer was in the area talking to residents and a few other people who mentioned the black truck I saw yesterday. Because I actually approached the truck and spoke to the man, Holderman wants me to come to his office to describe the man to a sketch artist. I told him that I'd do what I could."

"Yes, of course," Mom said.

"He mentioned that the little town where his office is located has a bunch of cute little shops all decked out for the holidays, as well as some pretty good restaurants. I thought maybe we could all go. You can go shopping while I meet with Holderman."

"I'd like to go," Bree said.

"Me too," Mom seconded.

"I think Tony and I will stay behind," I said when Mike turned to me. "We have the animals to think about. We don't know how long you'll be, and the dogs will need to go out again."

"Okay. Then it will be just the three of us," Mike said. "Holderman was going over to speak to someone named Hans Goober after he left here, so we arranged to meet in an hour."

"Who's he?" I asked.

"The closest resident to this house, and Holderman says he notices things. He's hoping he remembered seeing something on Friday night."

"Hans Goober must be the man Tony and I spoke to when we were looking for Leonard's owners that first morning here. He told us he spent winters at the lake, and he sounded as if he did see something."

"Like what?" Mike asked.

"He was sort of vague."

"Maybe Holderman can get more out of him. I have the feeling there could be something going on that we haven't stumbled upon yet. I'm going to run upstairs to change."

"Yeah, me too," Bree said.

"Text us when you know when you'll be back. If it's going to be late, Tony and I will start dinner."

Mom, Mike, and Bree, layered up to be warm while walking around the little town, and piled into Mike's truck and headed out. Before he left, Mike made a point of telling me to stay in the cabin, stay safe, and not to go sleuthing around on my own. Further proof, I decided, that my brother didn't know me at all.

"I'm assuming you aren't interested in Monopoly," Tony said after they left.

"You're assuming correctly. It seems to me if Doug Peterman was in the house when the killer arrived, as we suspect, and was killed for being here, there must be something going on that connects back in some way to this house or something that occurred in or near it."

"Agreed."

"I'd like to take a really good look around. I want to open all the drawers and cupboards, look for trapdoors and hidden compartments. If we don't find anything that stands out as being relevant, we'll head south and pay a visit to Conrad Bilson. The little store should be open from twelve to four today. I wanted to talk to him about my dad as well, so that's another reason to go."

"Okay, but this is a big house. Where do you want to start?"

"The seemingly empty conference room. My gut tells me it may not be as empty as it seems."

One of the things I love most about Tony is that he never balks or even hesitates when I ask him to do things that, on the surface, might seem slightly crazy. I get that my desire to investigate the death of a man who I don't know and whose death doesn't really affect me might not be the best use of my time off, but there's something about an unsolved murder, or any mystery for that matter, that gnaws at my gut and just won't leave me alone. I guess that's why I was like a dog with a bone when it came to finding the answers I sought in my dad's death or, more likely, it seemed, faked death. I liked things to be wrapped up nice and neat, and a state of ambiguity wasn't one I tolerated well.

"I don't know, Tess," Tony said when we entered the room. "This seems pretty empty."

I had to agree. There was a hardwood floor with an area rug under a large rectangular table. Chairs were placed around the table and a large monitor that measured at least a hundred inches on the wall, which was covered with pine paneling. Other than that, the room was barren. It did appear as if Peterman had locked himself in this room and then tried to climb out the window, but that didn't mean he had started off in this room. He might have seen a car pull into the drive, recognized the driver as someone he wanted to avoid, and ducked in here.

"This room feels odd to me," Tony said as he walked around the perimeter and checked the paneling for sections that might have been disturbed.

"Why is that?" I asked.

"The rest of the house is stick built, with a fairly large crawl space beneath the floor. I noticed when we walked around the exterior looking for Leonard the other night that while this room has the same log siding as the rest of the house, the foundation is built from cinder blocks. I suspect," Tony ran his hand over the wall, "that behind this paneling is cinder block all the way to the ceiling."

"So this room was built of cinder block, which was then paneled on both sides to disguise that fact. Why?" I asked.

Tony shrugged. "I would say it needed to be soundproof, or to provide extra security, but the existence of a hollow interior door and the addition of the window seems to negate that. I suppose it's possible the block structure already existed, and the house was built around it, incorporating the existing room into the new design. If that were true, Conrad Bilson should know what was here before the house."

"We'll ask him when we talk to him. Do you think there's something behind the monitor?" I asked. "If I was going to have a safe or a secret hiding space, I'd put it behind something like a picture or a monitor."

Tony walked over to the monitor. He ran his hands along the side, then put his face against the wall to try to take a peek behind it. "The unit is mounted to the wall. We'll need to lift this off, but it's going to be heavy."

"I'm not worried about the weight as much as the height." I looked at the clock on my phone. "Let's head over to the camp store. By the time we get there, Bilson should be open for the day."

******

Conrad Bilson was twenty minutes late opening the little store and attached laundromat that day, but it was his business, so I guess he was entitled to open it whenever he wanted. In a way, I was surprised he was open at all in the off season. Based on the hike we'd taken yesterday, looking for people who might have information about the pup or my dad, it appeared less than a third of the cabins were currently occupied.

"Can I help you?" Bilson asked as we walked in and came directly to the counter.

"I'm Tess Thomas. I'm staying in the house at the other end of the lake with my family."

"Yeah, I remember. Is there a problem?"

I shook my head. "No. I guess you heard we were the ones who found Mr. Peterman's body on our first day here. My brother, who's a police officer back home, is working with Officer Holderman on a few leads, but Tony," I nodded toward him, "and I have a few questions as well."

The man's eyes narrowed. "What sort of questions?"

"For one thing, we spoke to several long-term renters who seemed to think something odd was going on at the house."

"I wouldn't pay too much heed to what folks around here say. If you're looking for odd, consider the sort of person who would want to live all the way out here during the winter."

"You live out here during the winter," I pointed out.

He chuckled. "True. But I make my living here at the lake. Most of the folks who come back year after year with the intention of hunkering in until spring are loners who just want to be left alone. Which is a personal choice and perfectly fine, but the isolation does tend to get to some folks. Seems like there's always some sort of conspiracy theory going around. Last year, Hans Goober was sure the meteor he saw streak through the sky was an alien invasion, and two years ago, Cliff Farmer got everyone riled up about lights on the horizon. Personally, I think these little ideas give them something to talk about."

"Are all your long-term renters single men?" I asked.

"During the winter they are. Well, mostly. Tom Flanders used to be married, but his wife moved into town over the summer, and I haven't seen her since."

I remembered the photos of the woman with dark hair on the bookshelves.

"The rates for the cabins quadruple come late spring," Bilson continued. "The higher rates stay in place through the summer, so the winter residents mostly move on. There are one or two, like Tom Flanders, who have the financial means to live at the lake year-round."

"And Doug Peterson worked for you year-round?" I asked.

"He did. During the winter, it was just him. He mostly took care of repairs and cleaning for the short-term rentals. During the summer, his wife helps out with the cleaning. They'd been taking care of the cabins for the past eight years. He's going to be hard to replace."

"Did he live at the lake?"

Bilson shook his head. "No. He lived in town."

"I understand he was seen in town on Friday night at around eight. He mentioned he'd finished the work he had to do at the house. Yet he returned later. Did you call him with extra tasks to take care of?"

"No. There wasn't a lot to do. The Techucom folks had been at the house for a month before your stay. There was a tight turnaround because they didn't leave until Friday morning and you folks were arriving on Sunday. I told Doug he could take care of the place on Saturday, but he wanted to get started on Friday afternoon."

"I understand he never returned the key."

"That's right."

"And his truck wasn't at the house on Saturday?"

"No, it wasn't," he confirmed. "Is there a reason you're asking me all these questions?"

"Not really. We're just curious. I guess it's natural to be curious about the death of a man whose body you found."

Bilson tilted his head. "Yeah, I guess."

"I was wondering about the house itself," Tony said. "Do you happen to know if there was a structure built on the property before the house that's there now?"

"Sure was. Back when the lake was a base for a nearby mining camp, the camp office was located where the house sits today. It was a boxy place but sturdy. Built of cinder block to prevent robberies because the office doubled as a bank and held the safe where everyone's gold was kept."

"It appears the old office was built right into the new structure," Tony said.

Bilson nodded. "The old block building is part of the southeast corner of the house. Paneling was added to both the interior and exterior walls to give it a seamless look. I'm surprised you noticed the old building was still there. The interior walls are thicker in that part of the house. Guess you might have noticed that."

"I actually noticed the difference in the foundation," Tony said.

He nodded. "Ah. Yes, there's that as well. I was going to tear down the old bank and office when I decided to build the house to bring in a slightly higher-end clientele, but the history of the place got to me, so I just built around it."

I guessed that made sense. I was about to ask about the panel trucks when the phone rang and Bilson answered it. Judging by his side of the conversation, someone had called to inquire about cabin availability over the Christmas holiday. We'd asked pretty much what needed to be asked regarding Doug Peterman; now I needed to work my father and his friend Finn into the conversation.

"Sorry about that," he said after hanging up. "One of our repeat customers is thinking about spending some time here next month. Now, where were we?"

"Speaking of repeat customers, my dad used to come up here every year. His name was Grant Thomas. Do you remember him? It's been about fourteen years."

Bilson shook his head. "The name doesn't sound familiar."

"I understand he went by the name Tuck and came to visit someone named Finn."

He frowned. "Are you saying you're Tuck's daughter?"

"If this was the man who called himself Tuck." I held up the photo of my dad. Bilson took it and pretended to be studying it, but I saw an expression of recognition on his face right away.

Eventually, he said, "Yeah, that's him. Didn't know him well, but he seemed like a good guy. Listen, I need to get back to my inventory. It's been nice chatting with you both. Have a nice time while you're here."

He turned and went into the back room.

"Well, that was abrupt," I said.

"It seems we've been getting abrupt responses to all our inquiries about your dad. The general unwillingness to talk about him is making me even more curious about what might have happened here."

"Yeah." I let out a breath. "Me too. Let's go back to the house and take the dogs for a walk. I need to clear my head. The snow's let up a bit, but looking at the dark sky, I'd say the reprieve is most likely temporary."

Chapter 7

We bundled up in extra layers and set off along the forest trail with the three dogs. We'd already explored the trail that circled the lake during our fact-finding expedition, so we decided to see what was down the narrow path that had been created by the snowmobiles that left tracks leading into the dense grove of evergreens. It was a gorgeous walk. The fresh snow that had fallen covered the path just enough to make everything feel fresh but not so much to make it unnavigable. The firs that lined the path were heavy with snow, causing the branches to dip under the weight. I noticed small footprints in the snow. Fox, if I had to guess. I also noticed a few squirrels scurrying here and there. I felt myself relax as Tony's large hand surrounded my much smaller one. It was nice to spend time in nature without an agenda other than to enjoy the moment and the man I loved.

"It looks like Leonard is having the time of his life." Tony laughed as the pup bounced around between Titan and Tilly, attempting, it appeared, to get one of them to chase him.

"He really is. Talk about a bundle of energy. I think Mike might have his hands full with that one. He's either going to need to build a fence around his yard or bring the pup with him to work."

"He might make a good police mascot," Tony answered.

"He's pretty adorable. Bree could even take him with her to the bookstore once we get him trained not to bother people."

"Seems like the only one he really bothers now is Mike," Tony said.

I couldn't help but smile. "True. But Bree has breakable stuff in her shop, and with the holidays, she has all those decorations. Which reminds me: We still need to get a tree for the bookstore. There are some great ones out here. We'll need to come back before we head home. I wonder if we should get one for your house and my cabin as well."

"We have some pretty decent trees at home in White Eagle."

"That's true, and I'd prefer to wait a week or two to put up a tree. I kind of want to get the rest of the space decorated first, then add the tree last. Besides, the less time I have the tree in the cabin, the less time I have to struggle to keep the kittens from climbing it."

Tony smiled. "Yeah, there is that. I seem to remember having to pick both Tang and Tinder out of my tree last year. Of course, they were just kittens then. But I agree with focusing on the exterior decorations first and then moving inside to decorate the interiors, leaving room for the trees. I've been thinking about having a dinner party. A small one, once we get the decorations up in my place."

"That sounds perfect. I ran into Jordan Westlake on Friday, and we talked about getting together. I told him we'd have him out to your place for dinner, and I thought we'd invite Bree and Mike too. Oh, and Brady. I'm sure he'll fit in nicely with the others. He can bring Lilly or a date, if he prefers."

"And we'll need to invite Shaggy."

I scrunched up my nose. "Really? Jordan indicated he has someone he wanted to bring, so I was thinking this would be more of a couples thing."

"I'm sure Shaggy can get a date, and he is my best friend. It would hurt his feelings if we had a holiday dinner party and didn't invite him."

"Yeah. Okay. We'll ask Shaggy too. I'd worry about having Bree and Shaggy at the same table, but she'll be with Mike, so I'm sure it will be fine. Is Shaggy seeing anyone?"

Tony smiled. "I think he's seeing several someones. I'll make sure he asks someone who'll fit in with the rest of the group."

I put my arm through his and leaned my head on his shoulder. "Suddenly, I feel so grown-up, talking about decorating and dinner parties."

He laughed. "And you didn't feel grown-up before?"

"Not usually."

He kissed me on the top of the head. Snow flurries began to appear as we headed deeper into the forest, but I didn't mind. In a way, they added to the atmosphere of the early winter day. When Mom had first suggested this trip, my main focus had been on investigating my father's disappearance, but right now, as I walked through a winter fairyland with Tony and the dogs, that complicated mystery was the farthest thing from my mind.

We'd walked another ten minutes or so before Tony paused and tilted back his head to look into the sky. "I think the storm is going to intensify. We should head back."

"Okay. I'm getting kind of cold anyway." I called to the dogs. "Maybe when we get back, you can do a search on the computer to see what you can find out about Techucom."

"Why do you want to know about Techucom?" Tony asked.

I shrugged. "I can't quite get the idea out of my mind that whatever they were doing here could be related to Doug Peterman's death."

"I think that's highly unlikely. The group was gone before Peterman died. Besides, why would anyone from the company want to kill him?"

"I'm not saying someone from Techucom necessarily killed him, just that I'm interested in what they were doing up here."

"Okay. I can do a search if you'd like. All I have is my basic laptop with me, which has a search engine with limited capabilities, but I'm sure I can at least find some general information. The company was originally established in the mid-nineties by Talon Elton, who has an interesting background. He started off as a MIT-trained engineer with a serious gaming and hacking hobby who later honed his computer skills and went on to develop some cutting-edge technology that resulted in contracts with the federal government and the military."

"Which sounds like it could be a motive if Peterman stumbled on to the wrong thing."

"Again, highly unlikely. I don't know what might be behind Peterman's death, but I have the feeling it'll turn out to be something a lot more ordinary than a government cover-up."

"Like what?"

Tony shrugged. "Maybe Peterson got into a scuffle with someone at the bar who followed him when he left and killed him. We don't know the guy, but I don't think we should discount something as basic as a jealous husband or boyfriend. Peterson's wife has been out of town. Maybe Peterson was getting some on the side."

I wrinkled my nose. "I guess that makes as much sense as anything. Or maybe he liked to gamble and owed someone money, or he had a mistress who got tired of waiting for him to dump his wife." I looked at Tony. "I guess you make a good point that just because we believe he may have been at the house before his death doesn't mean we should assume the house or the people who had been staying in it are part of it."

When we returned to the house, Tony stoked up the fire while I made a pot of coffee. Then he went upstairs to get his laptop while I checked the cat boxes as well as all the water dishes. Mom had baked cookies at some point, and I put some on a plate and took them along with cups of coffee out to the dining table, where Tony had set up. The snow was getting harder. I hoped Mike and the others would be back shortly. I sort of doubted they'd want to spend too much time wandering around the shops in town in a storm. Still, it wouldn't hurt to text him to check in. Which I did shortly after settling in next to Tony at the dining table. "Ever hear of a man named Orson Hazelton?"

"He's another high-profile tech guy. He started Hazelton Technology six or seven years ago, which I believe focuses on guidance systems used by airlines. Why do you ask?"

"I just heard from Mike and he said the man he saw lurking in the area yesterday was driving a vehicle leased to him."

Tony frowned. "Are you saying it was Orson Hazelton Mike had the encounter with?"

I shook my head. "No. The man driving the vehicle wasn't Orson Hazelton. It seems someone provided the license plate number of the vehicle to Officer Holderman, and he was able to trace it to Hazelton. Mike says they're looking at employees of a company called Azeron Enterprises and comparing them to the sketch Mike helped the police artist come up with."

"Azeron Enterprises is another company owned by Hazelton. It's much smaller than Hazelton Technology and is focused on gaming rather than guidance systems."

I sat back and considered. "Seems like a lot of tech guys around. Maybe too many to be a coincidence."

"Maybe." Tony narrowed his gaze. "Give me a few minutes to check out a few ideas."

I nodded and picked up a cookie to nibble on until he found whatever it was he was looking for. My instinct was to chat while he worked, but I knew from past experience that when Tony was in the zone, it was best to sit quietly and wait. Though after three minutes I was bored to death, so I got up and went into the conference room to have another look around. I don't know why I was so certain there was something to find, but the little voice in my head that urged me to look again wouldn't quiet down, so I figured it wouldn't hurt to try one more time despite the fact that Tony and I hadn't found a thing that could be considered a clue when we'd looked before.

I stood in the middle of the room and considered the possibilities. I knew the walls were cinder block, so the odds of there being a secret room were slim. That basically left the table, chairs, and monitor. The monitor was mounted close to the wall and didn't look as if it would pull out, so that didn't give me a lot of options. On a whim, I forced my cheek against the wall and used the flashlight on my phone to peer behind the monitor. I didn't see anything, though I needed more height. I was using one of the chairs to stand on when I noticed something on the floor under the table. I bent down and picked it up. It was a single sheet of paper with a map drawn on it. At the top was a single word: *Verdeckt*.

I took the paper and walked back to where Tony was working. "What does *verdeckt* mean?"

Tony looked up. "It's German. It means hidden or concealed. Why?"

I help up the paper. "I found this on the floor in the conference room. What do you think it is?"

He took the paper from me. "It looks like a map." He studied the roughly drawn image in his hand, then pointed to a section of the drawing. "I think this is the lake, and this over here is the mountain behind it. If I had to guess, this is a map to something on the mountain."

"Like a mine?" I asked.

"I would say given that there are abandoned mines all over the place, that's as good a guess as any."

I walked around and stood behind Tony, who was still sitting at the table to get a better look at the map. "Okay, so what does the map lead to and do we think there's any possibility it's in any way tied to Doug Peterman's death?"

"I doubt it. For all we know, these are directions to a hiking trail. The group who was here before us was here for a month. I'm sure they got outdoors from time to time."

"Yeah. I guess you're right. Still, given the fact that a man is dead and this map was found on the floor of a locked room, I think we should show it to Mike."

"Absolutely."

"So, did you find anything?" I asked.

"Maybe." Tony paused and looked at me. "I don't know for certain this has anything to do with Doug Peterman, but I found out that Orson Hazelton used to work for Talon Elton. In fact, he was his right-hand man at one point. It seems the two had a falling out over some software Hazelton developed and Elton patented, which caused Hazelton to leave and start his own business. To say that the two men are bitter rivals would be putting it mildly."

"So maybe Hazelton sent his man to Timberland Lake to spy on Techucom and whatever they have going on, which required the presence of the panel trucks Tom Flanders told us about."

"Perhaps. The Techucom folks left on Friday and Mike saw the vehicle owned by Hazelton on Monday, so it's possible Hazelton is interested in the area for another reason altogether."

"Unless there's something that's remained behind, and that's what Hazelton is really interested in," I suggested.

"Like what?"

I lifted a shoulder. "I have no idea. I'm just spitballing. Did you find anything else?"

"There's some chatter on one of the dark web sites I sometimes poke around in that Hazelton is on the verge of announcing the launch of something that's going to rock the technology community, but I can't find a single mention of what that something might be. It's possible the whole thing is nothing more than a rumor. Unfounded speculation happens a lot on this particular site. If he does have something big on the horizon, I'm not sure why he would be messing around spying on his old boss and current nemesis."

"Unless he received some sort of intel that Techucom stole his idea," I mused. "He might be looking to confirm whether his project has been compromised."

"Maybe. But if the man in the truck was here to spy on Techucom, he was a few days too late."

"I guess that's true. Leonard is acting like he wants to go out. I think I'm going to take him."

"He just went."

I shrugged. "He's a puppy. Sometimes puppies forget to do what they're supposed to be doing when they go out and need to go again after they come in."

Tony laughed. "I guess so. I'll come with you."

We put on our outerwear, called to all three dogs, and headed outside. Once we'd left the yard, I stopped to look at Leonard. "Now would be the time to pee."

The dog cocked his head at me, then trotted over to a tree, where he proceeded to do just that. When he returned, we started around the house to the lake trail. It was then I noticed the footprints in the snow. "Hey, Tony, look at these."

He bent down for a closer look. "It appears as if the prints could have been made by the person who made the ones on the first night we were here." Tony stood up and looked in the direction of the footpath. "Let's follow them and see where they lead."

We followed the trail of footprints around the house to the lakeside. They seemed to stop at a short door, maybe four feet tall, under the back deck. It had a padlock that had been cut. We opened the door and stepped into the much-larger space where even Tony could stand. The height at the back of the house was the tallest, decreasing as you walked from the back toward the front of the house, eventually decreasing to the point where we'd be forced to crawl.

"I wonder who was down here and why?" I asked. "It looks like there are prints in the dirt in that direction." I pointed toward the front of the house, where a cinder block wall that went clear to the ground in one corner was clearly visible. "That must be the conference room."

"It's in the right spot." Tony shone his light around. "I guess whoever cut the lock had a look around. Let's take a look ourselves."

I followed Tony, who had to scrunch down after only a few steps. The scrunching was followed by squatting and, eventually, crawling. On the exterior of the cinder block wall, toward the bottom left corner were three symbols, which had been carved into the stone. "I recognize these," I said. "They're on the map I found."

Tony ran his finger over the shapes. "I think you're right." He took out his phone and snapped a photo.

"I bet whoever came down here was looking for the symbols."

"I don't know. This seems a little too *National Treasure* to me," he said, referring to a blockbuster movie from more than a decade ago. "I'm getting a kink in my neck. Let's head back the way we came. We'll go inside and clean up, then have another look at the map. Maybe we can figure out what the symbols mean. Maybe we can also figure out if the old mine office was represented on the map in the first place."

Tony and I crawled back to where we could stand, then headed to the exterior access door. After we made our way outside, we went inside to clean up and change into nondusty clothes. I made us some tea while Tony logged onto his computer. The map was opened up on the table next to him. I set both mugs of tea on the table, then sat down across from him. I picked up the map and took a closer look. There were some squares in the area surrounding the lake. They might represent buildings. Might all the buildings represented have symbols on them, and might the symbols provide clues to whatever was hidden?

Tony stopped typing, frowned, and sat back.

"This all feels off to me."

I picked up the map and looked at it again. "Maybe we should see what Mike has to say. He was going to try to see what Holderman knows. For all we know, he already knows about the map and what it might lead to." I ran my hand through my hair, which was still dusty from our trip under the house. "I could use a shower."

"I don't suppose you need help washing your back?"

I smiled. "Help washing my back seems like a very good idea."

Chapter 8

As it turned out, Mike and the others didn't return to the house until shortly before Tony had dinner ready. We decided not to discuss Doug Peterson's murder in front of Mom, who seemed stressed out enough, so we talked about the cute little town she and Bree had explored, and I commented on the cookies she'd baked, which were delicious. Once she headed into her suite, I could tell Mike about the map and Tony could catch us all up on whatever he'd discovered online. I hoped Mike had learned more about the man in the vehicle leased to Orson Hazelton and his reason for being at the lake.

"Ruthie called today to let me know Liza is having a baby in the spring," Mom informed us, referring to my Aunt Ruthie's daughter.

"Wow, another grandbaby," I said. "That makes four."

Mom looked pointedly at both Mike and me. "We have some catching up to do."

Mike threw his hands in the air. "Don't look at me."

"Me neither," I jumped in before Mom could focus her attention on me.

She didn't respond, but I could see that the subject of grandbabies had been on her mind. Tony and I had only been dating for a short time, so there was no way I wanted this conversation to continue.

Luckily, Mike chimed in with an alternate topic. "Mom and Bree found out about a festival the little town we visited today plans to hold on Friday. It's a hometown holiday sort of thing, with all the trimmings."

"It did look like fun," Bree jumped on the bandwagon. "All the little shops are going to be open and each one is going to sponsor a different wine as part of a progressive wine-tasting. I understand the wines from vineyards in Washington, Oregon, and Idaho are going to be the focus."

"There'll be appetizers and hot beverages as well," Mom added. "And the local merchants have done a wonderful job with the decorations. Every window along the main street had a display."

"Sounds like fun," I responded. "I'd love to go. We can look around, and maybe have lunch there. I might even be able to get a start on my Christmas shopping."

"When I was at the police station, Veronica, the receptionist, told me the town will also offer sleigh rides, either on wheels or runners, depending on the snow depth, as well as stands selling hot chestnuts, cider, and other seasonal food and drink," Mike added. "Oh, and there will be carolers as well."

"It sounded a lot like the Christmas Festival White Eagle holds closer to the holiday," Bree said. "I've always enjoyed that sort of thing."

"Speaking of the White Eagle Christmas Festival, I've been asked to rig up a sound system in the town square," Tony said. "They're going to have bands in the gazebo. I'm a bit worried about an outdoor event in December, but the committee assured me that they have tents they can put up, and portable fire pits they'll set around. Sounds cold to me, but it seems other winter destinations hold events like this all the time, and the turnout is really good."

"I suppose as long as you layer, it could be fun," I stated.

As the conversation naturally navigated to other towns who held outdoor concerts during the winter, I let my mind wander. I had so many things on my mind tonight—my dad, Doug Peterman's death, my mother's not-so-subtle hint about grandchildren—but the one topic that demanded the most space in my mind was the map I'd found and where it might lead.

I glanced out the window. The snowflakes that were illuminated by the deck lights seemed to indicate a treasure hunt—if that was what the map even led to—but that wasn't going to be in my immediate future. I didn't know the area, and the markers on the map were so vague as to be useless to anyone who was unfamiliar with the terrain, so heading out on a treasure hunt would be a dangerous endeavor whatever the weather. With the snow, it could be suicide. Though it was fun to think about a treasure hunt.

"Does that work for you?" Mike asked, staring directly at me.

"Uh. Sure. I guess so." I had no idea what I'd just agreed to; I'd ask Tony to fill me in later.

"Okay, then, it sounds like we have a plan," Mom said with a smile on her face.

I glanced at Tony, and he wasn't glaring at me with a look of indignation, so I probably hadn't just agreed to something like a grandbaby for Mom by this time next year.

"Mike and I will get the dishes tonight because you and Tony cooked," Bree offered.

"I think I'll head into my suite for a bath and some reading," Mom said. "I'll see you all in the morning."

After we said our good nights, Tony and I gathered the three dogs for a quick walk outdoors before we settled in for the evening.

"Okay. Break it to me gently. What did I agree to?" I asked after we'd left the house behind and headed down the narrow road.

"I didn't think you were listening."

"I wasn't, and I should have admitted it, but I panicked. When I was a kid, my mom always gave me a hard time for daydreaming when someone was speaking to me rather than listening to what was being said, so I hated to admit that was exactly what I was doing."

Tony wrapped my hand in his. "You can relax. All you agreed to was the time schedule for our trip to the festival on Friday."

I blew out a breath of relief. "That's good. The festival did sound like fun, and I really want Mom to have a wonderful week. She came to relax, but she looks stressed, and it's probably all my fault. I never should have asked her about my dad."

"It seems to me that your mom might have anticipated that the subject of your father might come up when she chose to come here."

"I guess that's true. I still wonder why she wanted to come here. She mentioned having unanswered questions, but she hasn't done a lot to resolve them."

"Maybe just being here and seeing what the lake is like was all she needed."

I shrugged. "Maybe."

"It's a shame the trip started off with a murder."

"I agree. Doug Peterman has been on my mind, and as hard as I try to let the local police handle the investigation, I find myself running theories in my mind."

"I guess it's natural to want to find an answer to a mystery that began when we found the body. Still, this isn't our mystery to solve."

I took a moment to respond. "That's true. And it would be nice to focus solely on gathering information about my dad's time at the lake. But for some reason, the complexity of this has grabbed me. I'm not sure which variables are linked to Peterson's death, but so far, we've found a map that may lead to a treasure or at least something valuable enough to draw a map to, and we suspect Techucom has been doing something downright stealthy up here."

"There does seem to be a lot going on," Tony responded.

"And now that we've filled Mike in about what we know about my dad, I have a feeling he's going to have more questions."

"I suspect he will."

"This hasn't turned out to be the sitting-in-front-of-the-fire-drinking-hot-cocoa sort of vacation I envisioned. I do find myself mentally stimulated by everything that has happened, though, and I'm enjoying our time together."

Tony turned me in his arms and kissed me gently on the lips. "Me too. But for your mom's sake, let's not discuss the Peterman case when she's around."

"Agreed."

By the time we returned to the house, Mike and Bree had finished cleaning the kitchen. We grabbed a bottle of wine and headed upstairs to the bedroom I shared with Tony, the farthest away from the room my mom occupied.

"Somehow, sneaking up here to talk so your mom won't overhear what we're saying feels like high school all over again." Bree laughed.

"Yeah, I guess it does," I said. "I'm afraid too much murder talk will ruin her vacation."

"I get that," Bree said. "She does seem like she's had a lot on her mind since we've been here."

I looked at Mike. "Did Officer Holderman track down the man you saw driving the vehicle leased to Orson Hazelton?"

Mike nodded. "His name is Ron Stinson and he works for Hazelton as a programmer. He told Holderman he's on vacation and drove out to the lake to meet up with some buddies but couldn't remember where the cabin was exactly. He decided to pull over to wait for one of his friends to show up."

I raised a brow. "Did Holderman check to see if his explanation was legit?"

"He did, and Stinson is staying in a cabin five or six down from this house with two friends who are up for the week."

"I suppose that means he isn't involved in Doug Peterman's murder. Did Holderman tell you who he thinks might be involved?" I asked.

"He shared a list of suspects he's following up with. Our conversation was cop-to-cop, which means if I share any of it with you, you have to promise not to speak of it in public or to approach the suspects or anyone related to them for any reason."

I glanced at Tony. He nodded. "Yeah, okay. What does he think is going on?"

"As far as Holderman can tell, Peterman was here on Friday afternoon, then left to go into town to go to a bar for a drink and some dinner. His wife is away, so he wasn't in a hurry to get home. He engaged in conversations with several locals. From what Holderman could uncover, Peterman was worried that evening about a man who used to date his sister but had since gone to prison. It seems he'd returned to town the day before and had been going around blabbing to everyone that he was back to square things up with the man who turned the cops on to the meth lab he was involved with."

"Peterman," I deduced.

"Exactly."

"Holderman tracked him down, and he seemed to have an alibi for the night of Peterman's murder. Holderman's keeping him on the suspect list for the time being; his alibi was a friend who very well might have lied for him."

"Was that his only suspect?" I asked.

"He had two others," Mike answered. "One was a local bookie Peterman owed a significant amount of money to, and the other was an old prospector who'd been telling anyone who would listen that Peterman stole a treasure map from him."

My eyes got big. "I found a map."

"What?" Mike asked.

I got up and walked across the room to the dresser, then handed the paper to Mike. "I found this today in the conference room."

Mike frowned as he looked at it.

"Did Holderman know anything about the map?" I asked.

"He just said there's a local legend about a man who robbed a bank back in the nineteen forties and hid the money up here in one of the abandoned mines when he was forced to ditch the money to escape the sheriff, who was close to catching up with him."

"So, if the legend is true, maybe the map is legit," Bree said.

"This map looks new and the money was stolen three quarters of a century ago," Mike pointed out. "Still, the map you found could have been a copy of it. That still doesn't explain why it was found in the conference room, though."

"Maybe Peterman copied the map and had it on him when he came back here last Friday," I suggested. "If he did lock himself in the conference room, maybe he dropped this when he was looking for a way out."

"I suppose it might have gone down that way," Mike said. "Whatever the explanation, I need to call Holderman. I'm sure he'll want to stop by to pick this up. I hate to bother Mom, so perhaps I'll arrange to meet him out on the road."

I looked longingly at the map. Goodbye, treasure hunt. Not that the map or even the legend were necessarily legit. And not that it was practical to head out looking for a lost mine anyway. I'd already come to that conclusion. Mike giving the map away was probably a good thing. It might be the action that would turn out to prevent me from ignoring my common sense and doing something stupid.

Chapter 9

Wednesday, November 21

The first thing I noticed when I awoke the next morning was that it had snowed again. A lot. Too much, I decided, to be out tromping around in it. Not that the dogs wouldn't need to go out, but we could walk on the road or maybe wear down a path near the house. Tony and our dogs weren't in the room, so I assumed he'd woken early and taken them out. I slowly stretched my arms up over my head. The fire was burning warmly in the fireplace and the room was toasty warm.

I snuggled under the fluffy down comforter for a few more minutes before rolling out of bed. Tomorrow was Thanksgiving, and Mom had been making noises about baking rolls as well as pies and making some of the sides that would keep a day. Thanksgiving morning was a traditional time for her homemade sticky rolls, which I figured she'd make today and reheat tomorrow.

Thinking of food made me think of coffee, so I tossed off the comforter and sat up. Then, pulling on a clean pair of jeans, a long-sleeved shirt, and a hoodie, I slipped my feet into my fuzzy slippers and headed into the bathroom to brush my teeth and comb my hair. With that accomplished, I headed downstairs, where I could hear talking.

"Morning," I said to Bree and Mom as I headed across the room to the coffeepot.

"Morning, sweetheart. How did you sleep?" Mom asked.

"Really well. Where are Mike and Tony?"

"Tony's outside getting wood for the fireplace and Mike took the dogs for a walk," Bree said.

"Mike took all three dogs for a walk."

"You sound surprised."

"I guess I am. But I'm grateful as well. Not having to get up with the dogs let me sleep in a bit." I looked around the room. Tang and Tinder were both on the giant dog bed that was in front of a little woodburning stove. "I guess I should feed the cats."

"Tony took care of that before he went out," Mom informed me. "He cleaned the cat boxes too."

Suddenly, I was feeling very spoiled. A morning without chores wasn't a bad thing. I topped off my coffee, then slid onto one of the stools at the counter. "What are you making?" I asked Mom.

"Right now, I'm making the dough for the rolls for tomorrow night's dinner. I figure with the cool, damp weather, the dough might take a while to rise. After that, I'm going to make an egg pie for breakfast. Do you think I should do bacon or sausage?"

"Either is fine with me," I answered.

"I don't mind frying up some of each," Bree offered. "I was going to cut up some of that melon as well."

I knew I should offer to help, but I was enjoying this slow start to my day. I'd offer to do the dishes when we'd eaten. I'd be fully awake then and raring to do something,

I was just about to pour my third cup of coffee when Mike walked in with all three dogs. They'd brought in quite a bit of snow with them, so I changed direction and went for the mop. "How was your walk?" I asked.

"Eventful."

I raised a brow. "Would you care to elaborate?"

"I was walking down the road when Leonard took off after a rabbit. I called him back, but he wasn't listening. I tried to keep up with him, but the road was slick and I fell on my backside. Of course, once I was sprawled on the ground, Leonard thought we were playing a game and came running over to jump on me and lick my face."

It was very hard to suppress a grin as Mike continued.

"Somehow," he glared at the puppy, who was sitting on his foot and looking at him adoringly, "I managed to get up without slipping again. It was about then that a man came walking down the road with two exceptionally well-trained dogs, making my hellion appear to be even more undisciplined."

"He's just a puppy," I said. "He'll learn to resist the urge to chase rabbits and come when he's called."

"I hope so. And Tilly and Titan were total angels, which helped me save face. Anyway, this man and his two dogs came walking down the road. Leonard ran right up to him, and he said his name was Walton Young and he lived two doors down from this house on the west side of the lake. He'd been out of town and had just returned last night. We walked together for a while and chatted along the way. It seems he hadn't heard about Doug Peterman, so I filled him in with the information I was certain was public knowledge. I mentioned that several folks had talked about strange things going on when the Techucom folks were in town, and that more than one person suspected Peterman had seen something he shouldn't have. Young was doubtful, so I mentioned the panel trucks and strange lights at the house, and he said the trucks were used to transport lasers and large telescopes. He didn't know what Techucom might be doing with lasers, but they seemed to be doing it at night."

"We know they do stealthy government stuff," Bree said. "If they were doing something with lasers it wouldn't surprise me."

"And Young said the panel trucks left with the lasers a couple of days after they arrived. Lasers and giant telescopes are a bit out of the norm for this area, but in Young's opinion, there wasn't anything going on here that would result in Peterman being shot."

"Did he have an opinion on why he was?" I asked.

"No, but he said Peterman didn't always get along with all the people in the area. Young went out of his way not to finger anyone specifically as being a suspect, but he did mention Hans Goober, who has an active imagination and was telling everyone Peterman had stolen his map. I didn't mention that we'd found a map. Young also said Goober has seen the Techucom men shooting off the lasers late at night and was convinced they were aiming at aliens, that the other locals were under attack and needed to defend the area. There were some who tried to explain there were no aliens, and the Techucom team was doing some sort of test or experiment, but he didn't believe them. The guy sounds like a real nutcase and owns a rifle, so I suggested Young call Holderman to fill him in on what he knew. He said he would."

"Did this Walton Young have any other theories?" Mom asked as she slipped a baking pan into the oven.

"He did say Peterman and his wife had been having problems, and that it was his understanding she wasn't just visiting her sister but that she had taken the kids and moved in with her after she found out he'd been having an affair. According to Young, the woman Peterman was sleeping with was also married. It was Young's opinion that the husband of this woman might have found out that Peterman was sleeping with his wife and taken matters into his own hands."

"That sounds like as good a motive as any," Mom said.

"Young seemed to know who Peterman had been having the affair with but didn't say. What smells so good? I'm starving."

"Egg pie. Why don't you go out to tell Tony that breakfast is almost ready, and then both of you can wash up."

******

After breakfast, I made good on my intention and did the dishes. Tony volunteered to help me, so Mom, Bree, and Mike went into the living room. While we ate, we'd discussed the side dishes Mom was considering putting together, so I figured once we finished cleaning the kitchen, we'd end up messing it up again, but it was a good idea to at least start off with a clean space.

"What do you think about the idea that Doug Peterman was having an affair?" I asked Tony.

"It makes a better motive for murder than any of the others we've explored, but it leaves unanswered questions too. Like why did he come back out to the house after he was in town? Why did he flee, assuming he did try to escape through the window? Where's his truck? It sounds as if he drove it to the lake, and it was seen parked in front of the house, so where is it now?"

"I wonder if looking for the truck might be a good next stage of investigation," I said. "Find the truck, find the killer."

"Maybe, but how do we find the truck?"

"If the truck is new, it could have a GPS system. If it doesn't, it seems reasonable that someone noticed it drive by on the way to and from the house. The road around the lake isn't busy. Headlights would be something someone might take notice of."

"If the person who killed Peterman drove his truck away, what did they do with their own vehicle?" Tony asked.

"Maybe they didn't have one. Maybe they were already here. Or maybe the killer came to the lake with Peterman."

Tony lifted a brow. "Do you care to elaborate?"

"Maybe Peterman was in town, chatting with various people, and struck up a conversation with someone, which led him to come back here. Maybe that someone came with him. At some point, Peterman realized that person wished him ill and tried to flee. The person shot him and then drove the truck back to town."

"Seems a bit far-fetched; possible, but unlikely. It does make me wonder about the gun. We know Peterman was shot. If he was shot here at the lake, why didn't the residents closest to this end of it hear anything?"

"Good question," I answered.

"Is it possible Peterman was shot elsewhere, then brought here and dumped in the water?"

"It's possible, but it wouldn't explain the window."

"What if the open window has absolutely nothing to do with the murder? What if he opened it when he was cleaning but forgot to close it? What if the screen was off because he removed it to wash the window? Or maybe someone from Techucom removed it and Doug never got around to putting it back. Maybe Peterman remembered the window was still open after he'd gone to town and that was why he returned?"

"Then why was the door to the conference room locked?" I asked.

"Maybe it happened accidentally. I have no idea, but I think it might be a good idea not to get too locked in to the theory that he opened and escaped out that window."

"Okay, so if not how, it seems we're back to why. Things just aren't adding up. I feel like we're missing something. We have theories about why Peterman might have come back and theories about why the window might have been open, but there are too many unknowns for a solution to be anywhere in sight."

"Again, I'm going to suggest this isn't our murder to solve. Officer Holderman is working on it. This is his home ground. He knows the players in a way we can't. Tomorrow is Thanksgiving. I say we take a step back and let him do his job while we spend a nice holiday with your family."

"You're right. It would be nice to just relax."

Of course, just relaxing was going to be harder than I thought with Mike involved in the investigation. I was just wiping down the counters when he came in to let me know he'd spoken to Holderman about his conversation with Walton Young, and the officer had some concerns about it. He wanted to speak to Mike in person, so Mike volunteered to go into town and Bree went with him. That left Tony and me to help Mom with the rolls, pies, and sides, though there was only so much room in the kitchen, which was probably for the best anyway.

"It's snowing again," Tony said as he diced apples.

"It's pretty," I said, and glanced at the cheery fire. "And cozy."

"I'm enjoying things," Mom said, "although I'm sorry Mike keeps getting pulled away to work on the murder case. I realize he's a police officer and getting pulled away comes with the territory, but he's on vacation. I hoped he would be able to relax."

"I guess it's hard not to bring who you are with you when you venture away from home. Are you thinking one or two pumpkin pies?"

"Two. Everyone will want pie with the leftovers. I planned to make two pumpkin and two apple." Mom opened the refrigerator and looked inside. "Oh, dear."

"What's wrong?" I asked.

"We're going to be short on butter if we make four pies."

I glanced at the clock. It was almost noon. "The store will be open in a few minutes. I'll run down and get some. How much do you need?"

"Maybe two pounds."

"I'll go with you," Tony said, untying his apron. "Do you need anything else?"

Mom adjusted things inside the refrigerator. "You might want to grab some eggs and milk as long as you're there. I doubt the store will be open tomorrow, and I'd hate to run short."

Tony and I bundled up and headed out to his truck. The drive to the camp store would be slow with all the snow, but I didn't mind, though the way the road wound away from the lake along the eastern shore made it almost quicker to walk when the weather wasn't bad.

"It looks like the storm is starting to break up. At least temporarily. We should take the dogs for a long walk if it does. It might be a good idea to work off some of their energy just in case the weather turns bad again."

"I'm game," Tony said. "It's been nice spending time with your family, but I feel like I have some excess energy to burn as well."

"With all the wood you've chopped, I'm surprised you aren't exhausted."

"I guess living and working alone, you get used to the quiet. There hasn't been a lot of that while we've been here. Not that I'm not having fun. It's just that a walk would be nice."

The lights were on inside the store, indicating it was open when we pulled up. Tony parked near the entrance and we piled out and walked to it.

"Afternoon, folks," Conrad Bilson said as we went in.

"Afternoon," I replied.

"Did you notice the sign that says the store will be closed tomorrow and Friday? I'll be open on Saturday, though."

I nodded. "I saw. Are you going somewhere for the holiday?"

"My daughter lives in town. I usually spend Thanksgiving with her family."

I smiled. "That's nice. Family is important."

"It is, and mine is the best. My girl has an open-door policy to anyone who needs a place to go. I usually take one or two people from the lake with me."

"Who are the lucky men this year?"

"I've invited Tom Flanders. He's recently separated and could use the company. I also invited Luke Conners. I'm not sure whether you've met him. He lives in the little cabin about halfway up the road on the west shore of the lake."

I shook my head. "No, I don't think we've met him."

"He's a nice guy. A little down on his luck, but a nice guy." Bilson glanced away from me and cleared his throat. "Listen, as long as you're here, I have something I wanted to tell you."

I walked closer to the counter he was leaning on. "Okay."

"When you were in the other day asking about Finn and your father, it caught me off guard. I know I didn't respond well, but I didn't have time to think and I guess I panicked."

"So you do know something," I prompted.

He nodded. "It's a secret I've kept for a long time. I'm not sure I should be telling it now. Maybe it's the holiday that's making me sentimental, but I've asked around a bit, and from what I've been able to find out, it seems you're pretty intent on getting your answers."

"I am." I wanted to snap at him to hurry up and say it already, but I knew I needed to be patient if I wanted him to continue. "I've been looking for answers about my father's death for years. If you know something, it would mean the world to me if you'd share it with me."

"I don't know everything," he warned. "I'm not even sure what I know is the truth. But after Finn was shot, your dad and I shared a bottle of scotch to commemorate a man we both knew and respected, and secrets were shared."

I could physically feel my heart quicken. "I'm listening."

Conrad Bilson cleared his throat. "It seems your dad was living something of a secret life. I don't

117

know all the details, but apparently he was in the witness protection program at some point. I don't know what he'd seen. I don't know when he entered the program, and he never said who he was before that, but he did say that the one rule he'd absolutely been sworn to was never to tell anyone the truth about his past, and even more importantly, he was to cut all ties to it. That night, it was that rule he admitted he'd broken. It was something he regretted doing."

Witness protection had been my first guess after we'd learned what we had about my dad, but it was still surprising to hear someone say it out loud. And I was surprised to hear he'd broken the rule. He'd never said a word to us about his past or the people he'd known. "Finn," I mused.

Bilson nodded. "He said Finn was the only person he'd hung on to from his old life. He thought it would be fine. He figured they'd meet up here in private and no one would ever find out. But when Finn was shot with a high-powered sniper rifle, your dad knew he'd been wrong. He suspected he was the reason Finn had died."

"He must have been devastated."

"I'd say Finn's death hit him hard. I don't know how he and your dad were connected, but I figured in order for him to make an exception to what seemed to be an important condition of his relocation, Finn must have been very important to him."

I was sure Bilson must be right about that.

"Your dad told me that he was a dangerous man to know. He vowed as we sat under the stars, drinking to Finn, that he was going to cut out of his life everyone who might get hurt because of him. Shortly after that, I heard he was killed in a truck accident. I don't know if the accident was his way of keeping that promise to himself, but I always wondered."

I glanced at Tony. I think we both suspected the accident was to make the man without a past disappear again.

"Thank you," I said. "It means a lot to me that you were willing to share this with me."

"Bit of advice," Bilson said.

"Sure."

"If you've been going around stirring things up, you might want to stop. If your dad didn't die—if he chose to disappear to protect you—by looking for him, you're wiping out his sacrifice by putting yourself in danger anyway. From the little I knew of him, that's the last thing he'd want."

Conrad Bilson was right. That was the last thing he'd want. I had my answer. At least one of them. I had no idea what he was doing now, but I supposed I had enough. Maybe I really should just leave it alone. I thanked Bilson again, and Tony and I went back out to the truck.

"What do you think?" Tony asked with an obvious tone of caution in his voice.

"I don't know. The explanation Bilson provided is something I'd mostly worked out on my own. It makes sense based on everything we've learned. And he wasn't wrong when he said my dad would want me to leave it alone."

"I think so too."

"Of course, now that we've brought Mike in on things, I'll have to see if he agrees. I think I might be willing to let it go and get on with my life. If Mike feels the same way, of course. If not, I guess we'll need to talk about things until we can settle on something we all can live with. We'll talk tonight."

"And your mom?" Tony asked.

"I'll talk to Mike first, but I think we should tell her. She has the right to know."

******

Later that evening, after Mom retired to her suite, I told Mike and Bree I had something to talk to them about in my room. As they had on other evenings this week, they grabbed a bottle of wine and met us in the seating area of the suite, near the fireplace.

"What's up?" Mike asked.

"I have news about Dad. It's kind of a long story, so let me get through what I know before you say anything."

A look of caution crossed Mike's face. "Okay."

I started at the beginning, sharing what Conrad Bilson had said about Dad and Finn and the night they'd shared a bottle in memory of a dear friend. I told them that Bilson didn't think Dad would want us looking for him, and that after thinking things through, I agreed with his opinion. Then I waited for Mike's reply.

When he didn't speak for a moment, I began to become concerned. When he did speak, his reply wasn't at all what I was expecting. "What if he is lying?"

I frowned. "Lying?"

"What if everything Bilson told you is a lie to try to convince you to give up your search for our dad? What if Dad didn't disappear voluntarily? What if he was forced? What if he is trapped in some sort of a horrible situation and hopes someone will find him and set him free?"

I glanced at Tony and quickly saw he was going to let me handle this. "I don't think that's what's going on. The idea of being in witness protection fits everything we know to this point. And from the photos we've found since the supposed truck accident, it doesn't appear he's being held against his will. It looks like he has the freedom to move around. I know you haven't had the time I've had to process everything, but what Bilson said makes sense."

Mike bowed his head and ran his hands through his hair. I could see he was deeply affected.

I got up and sat down next to him, then put my hand on his arm. "Look, we don't have to decide anything tonight. Let's all sleep on it and talk again in a day or two. I'm struggling with whether to bring Mom in on all this, but even if we decide to, I don't want to do it tomorrow. Tomorrow we're going to have an old-fashioned family Thanksgiving. Anything else can wait until Friday."

Chapter 10

Thursday, November 22

There's nothing better on a cold, snowy day than Mom's sticky buns, crisp bacon, scrambled eggs, and mimosas next to a roaring fire. Tony had taken the dogs out for a very quick walk, but even they seemed content to sleep by the fire while we sipped champagne and orange juice and coffee and gave thanks for the time we had together.

I'd slept surprisingly well despite the fact that I had my conversation with Mike on my mind. I wondered if involving him in my secret had been the right thing to do. The timing definitely could have been better. If I'd had any idea when I'd shared my news about our father's possible lack of deadness that a few short days later I'd all but decide to let sleeping dogs lie, I would never have opened a door I wasn't sure I'd be able to close.

I felt bad that Mike looked as if he hadn't slept a wink. He was supposed to be at the lake on vacation, but between Doug Peterman's murder and Mike's continued involvement in it and the news I'd shared about Dad, he'd probably have gotten more rest and relaxation if he'd stayed home and worked his regular shift.

Mom had gotten up early to put the turkey in the oven. She'd made the coffee and started all the fires. I could see she at least was excited about the day ahead. I was glad we'd made most of the food for our Thanksgiving dinner the day before so we could all relax today. Someone, I think Bree, had pulled out a couple of board games and set them on the sofa table in the main living area. Tony offered to dig out the hot tub so anyone who wanted to take a soak would have easy access to the warm water as the snow drifted slowly from the sky, and Mike had mentioned bringing a full day's worth of wood inside so we didn't have to keep going out onto the covered porch to restock the two woodburning fireplaces on the first floor.

"The Macy's parade should be on TV," Mom said. "I'd like to watch it for a while if no one minds."

"I like to watch the parade every year," Bree said.

"Yeah, me too," I agreed.

"I'm fine with it until the game starts," Mike added.

"And I'm fine with whatever everyone else would like to do," Tony topped it off.

Mom turned on the flat-screen television, then used the remote to change the channel. A commercial for one of the popular cell-phone carriers popped onto the screen. Suddenly, I wondered if Doug Peterman's phone had been on him when his body was found. He'd been in the water, so I wasn't sure the phone would still be operational. Probably not. Still, his phone records would indicate if he'd spoken to anyone during the last hours of his life.

Mom pointed to one of the balloons that made the Macy's Thanksgiving Day Parade so popular. I smiled and made an appropriate reply, although my attention had moved on to Peterman's truck. It did seem like knowing where it was could provide us with clues to who'd killed him. I thought about my conversation with Tony yesterday, and my comment that maybe the killer was already at the lake when Peterman came back to take care of a forgotten chore, like closing the window. We didn't know of any married men in town, but what if the motive for the murder was something other than an alleged affair. Might one of the locals have seen Peterman arrive and used his presence so late in the evening to confront him about whatever the motive turned out to be?

Hans Goober came to mind. He was only a couple of cabins away, and it did seem as if he wasn't fully in control of his mental faculties. My thoughts wandered to the map. After Mike turned it over to Officer Holderman, I hadn't given it a lot of thought, but what if it did lead to a treasure?

"Something on your mind?" Tony asked.

I smiled. "Not really. Just daydreaming. It's cozy sitting here watching the parade while it snows."

"The view from this window is pretty great," Tony said.

"I like the view," Mom said, "but I don't really like sitting in here after dark. Those big windows looking out on the lake make me think the cabins across the lake can look right in here when it's dark outside but the lights are on inside."

Mom made a good point. If Peterman had turned on the lights when he'd come back last week, the people in the cabins across the lake would have been able to see that he was here. I thought about Tom Flanders, who'd informed us that he'd seen the lights on inside the house late at night when the Techucom folks were here. If Doug Peterman was here and Tom Flanders was home, wouldn't he have at a minimum seen the lights on that night as well? It seemed another conversation with him might be in order. Of course, he was having Thanksgiving with Conrad Bilson and his daughter today, so it would have to wait.

Maybe if the snow stopped I'd take the dogs for a walk around the lake and stop by for a chat with Hans Goober. He'd been pretty tight-lipped before, but I suspected he knew something. I could take him a piece of pie. We had tons, and I imagined he'd enjoy a slice of homemade pumpkin.

I was working on my strategy to get out of the house with a piece of pie without drawing suspicion that my intention was more than just a neighborly urge when Tony suggested we take the dogs out. I supposed that was as good a reason as any to sneak away for a few minutes. I grabbed a slice of pie and wrapped it in tinfoil, then bundled up to set out into the snowy day.

"Is there a reason we have pie?" Tony asked.

"I was going to drop a piece off to Hans Goober."

"Seems like a nice thing to do. He's probably alone today."

I felt my heart sink at the thought. "Yeah. You're probably right. It did sound as if he was mostly alone in the world."

As we approached Goober's cabin, I noticed wood smoke circling up from the chimney. I told the dogs to stay and approached the front door and knocked.

"Yeah?" he answered.

I held out the paper plate with the pie on it. "Happy Thanksgiving. I brought you a piece of pie. I hope you like pumpkin."

His eyes softened just a bit. "You brought me pie? Why?"

"We had plenty, and I thought you might enjoy some."

He took a step back. "Come on in. I have something for you too."

I glanced at Tony, who stood near the dogs. He shrugged, and I turned back to Hans. "Okay. But just for a minute. I have Tony and the dogs with me."

The room was small and cluttered. I suspected the last time it had been cleaned was when Doug Peterman did it before Hans moved in for the winter. Hans walked over to the stove. He spooned something from a pot into a tin cup. "This here is elk stew. It's tasty."

"It looks delicious, but I just ate breakfast."

"You can take it with you and bring the cup back later. As long as you're going to have to come back anyway, I wouldn't mind a slice of turkey to go with the pie you brought."

"I think that can be arranged. I'll stop back with a whole plate with trimmings and all."

"I like gravy."

"I'll bring extra gravy."

I turned to leave when I noticed a map that looked a whole lot like the one I'd found in the conference room sitting on a table near a well-worn chair. "I've seen that map before."

"Leads to a treasure. My grandpappy gave it to me a long time ago."

"You must be the prospector who had his map stolen."

"Yeah, that was me. I got it back, though."

"I saw a copy of this map on the floor in the house we're renting. Did you know there were copies?"

Hans narrowed his gaze. "Can you keep a secret?"

"Sure. I guess."

"My grandpappy gave me this map when I was ten years old. For a long time, I didn't do a thing with it other than stash it away with some old photos. Then, twenty years ago, I decided to try to find the treasure. I've spent every summer for the past twenty years doing just that. Talk about a waste."

"I guess you didn't find it."

"I've come to the conclusion there isn't a treasure to find. I finally made some money off this old map, however."

I raised my eyes. "How did you do that?"

"It was Doug's idea, really. He said he needed money to pay off his bookie and he had an idea how he could get the money he needed and I could get some money too. I told him I was interested, so he explained his plan. I let it be known my map had been stolen and I was real mad about it because I was close to finding the treasure. Meanwhile, Doug took the map and had it copied. He let it slip out that he was the one who had stolen the map and was willing to sell copies for the right price. That boy was a genius. He found ten people to buy a copy of this old map for five hundred dollars apiece. He gave me my cut last week."

"So you're saying there are ten people with this map who'll be sneaking around looking for the clues on the map?"

Goober shrugged. "Yeah, I guess so."

"We noticed someone recently got into the crawl space under the house we're renting."

"I guess they were looking for the symbols that were carved into the old mining office. There used to be symbols carved into a lot of the buildings around here, but most of them have been torn down."

"So you and Doug conned ten innocent people?"

"I wouldn't say we conned them. Doug offered to sell them a map, which he did. He never guaranteed that all the clues led to things that still existed. And he never promised anyone they'd be successful in their treasure hunt. Besides, even without all the clues, one of the scientist types who were up at the lake this past month might have figured out a way to find the treasure without the symbols, so the maps do have the potential to do what they suggest they might do."

I rolled my eyes. Talk about a con. Still, it didn't look as if Hans killed Doug Peterman, and I doubted that one of the Techucom employees who fell victim to Doug's scam killed him over a five-hundred-dollar map they wouldn't even have had time to attempt to follow. I said goodbye and returned to where Tony was waiting.

"You went in with pie and came out with... coffee?"

"Elk stew."

"Sounds interesting." Tony took my hand and began to walk away from the cabin and back toward the house.

I glanced at the tin mug Tony held. "I told Hans I'd bring him a plate of food when I return the mug. I feel bad for him. He really does seem to be all alone in the world."

"I suppose his being alone is his choice, but I see what you mean."

The first thing I noticed when we arrived at the house was the police car in the drive. "Oh, this can't be good."

"It's probably Officer Holderman come to talk to Mike," Tony said.

"Yeah, probably. I think it's a little odd that he keeps seeking Mike out to the extent he has. In the television shows I watch, the cops are always so territorial."

"Mike is a likable guy who knows his stuff. I'm sure Holderman is happy to have his input. Let's take the dogs in through the kitchen so we can dry them off a bit before we give them the run of the house."

The kitchen was empty when Tony and I went in, but I could smell the turkey in the oven. and oh boy did it smell good. We grabbed a stack of towels from the laundry room and set to drying all three dogs as best we could. We were just about finished when Bree walked in.

"I didn't hear you guys come in."

"We wanted to dry off the dogs so we came in the back door," I told Bree. "Is Holderman here?"

"He's talking to Mike in the conference room. I came in to check the turkey and grab some tea. Your mom and I are watching a tape of one of the other parades while Mike is busy with Holderman. I'm sure he'll commandeer the television for football when he's finished with his conversation."

"I like football," I said.

Tony set the tin mug on the counter. I took another look at the stew. It seemed fine, but I couldn't help but remember how filthy the cabin was. I dumped the stew down the drain and ran the disposal. I'd just tell Hans it was delicious when I returned the mug.

"Is there anything we need to do now other than keep an eye on the bird?" I asked.

"Nope; everything is ready to heat when it's time. Come in and relax. We'll watch some football and drink some tea."

"If we're watching football, I think I'll go with beer." I looked at Tony. "Want one?"

"Sure. Beer and football do go together."

"It sounds like Holderman is leaving," Bree said.

I followed her into the living room. Mike was showing the officer out.

"What was that all about?" I asked after the squad car drove away.

"Holderman's on his way to pick up Hans Goober. Tom Flanders from down the lake reported that he saw Doug Peterman go over to Hans's place after he came back here the night he died. He was shot shortly after that. I guess Holderman figured out that the map we gave him was a copy of the one Goober reported having been stolen and put two and two together."

I frowned. "I just spoke with Hans Goober. Doug Peterman didn't steal the map. Goober started that rumor as part of a plan the two men had to copy and sell the map."

"Even if that's true, it looks like Goober was the last one to see him alive."

It was odd he hadn't mentioned Peterman coming by on Friday night. It was odder still that he'd seemed to be legitimately surprised when I told him Doug Peterman was dead.

Chapter 11

Dinner, in a word, was perfect. The fire crackled merrily as huge flakes of fluffy white snow drifted toward the ground. The food was some of the best I'd ever eaten, and the conversation somehow managed to avoid death and drama and remain firmly on family memories and upcoming holiday plans. It really was the very best holiday meal I'd had in a very, very long time. In fact, the whole thing was so lovely that thoughts of Doug Peterman's murder didn't penetrate my mind until I came across Goober's tin mug in with the other dishes.

I wondered if he'd been arrested. It made me sad to think that he'd spend the holiday in jail. Maybe I'd walk over and take a peek. If he was home, I'd bring him the plate of food I'd promised. Maybe I'd make one up and take it with me just in case.

When I arrived at his cabin, I found the place deserted. I felt a sadness in my heart as I retraced my steps despite the fact that just a few hours earlier I'd thought he might be guilty. Peterman stopping at Goober's seemed to negate the idea that he had locked himself in the conference room to avoid someone and fled out the window in an ill-fated attempt to get away. If that hadn't been what happened, what had?

"Goober not at home?" Tony asked when he saw me return with the mug and the plate of food.

"No. I guess Holderman must have taken him in. I'll admit I thought he might be guilty given the timeline of events, but now my gut is telling me he's innocent."

"If he didn't do it, who did?" Tony asked.

"I'm not sure. We know Peterman was here to clean earlier in the day. We know he went into town for a meal and a drink but came back here later for some reason. We suspect he was in this house when he found the need to escape someone, so he locked himself in the conference room, then left through the window. The fact that he took the time to stop by Goober's place seems to negate the fact that he was running from someone. Yet he died not long after Tom Flanders saw him show up at Goober's place and the location where his body was found wasn't all that far away from it."

"Which brings us back to the gunshot no one seemed to have heard," Tony pointed out.

"There is that. The sound of gunfire would have carried. Every cabin on this lake would have been within the sound range, and yet not one person we've spoken to has mentioned hearing it. I guess the killer could have used a silencer. I doubt Hans Goober has a gun with a silencer. The only gun I noticed in his cabin was an old hunting rifle."

Tony took my hand and led me over to the kitchen counter. He indicated that I should take a seat. "Are you sure you want to do this today?"

"Want? No. Not really. But I think I need to figure this out. If Goober is innocent, it's so sad he's spending Thanksgiving in jail."

Tony sat down next to me. "Let's go over this again. We know Tom Flanders called to tell Holderman he saw Peterman go over to Goober's cabin on the night he died. He must have seen it on Friday and this is Thursday of the following week, so why do you think he took so long to say anything?"

"Good point. Why wouldn't he have mentioned it the day he heard Peterman had been shot and his body had been found in the lake?"

"Maybe something happened today that got him to finally speak up," Tony suggested.

"Like what?"

"I don't know. But another question that should have occurred to us long before this just occurred to me. Based on our current theory, Peterman was shot and killed on Friday night. We've been operating under the assumption that his body ended up in the lake shortly thereafter. Yet we didn't find his body until late Sunday afternoon."

My eyes grew big. "So why didn't someone stumble across his remains before we did?"

"Exactly. Maybe we should bring Mike into this discussion. He might know more than he's told us."

"Okay. Let's see if we can pull him away from his pie hangover long enough to discuss the situation."

Mike was in a mellow mood thanks to all the food and wine he'd consumed. He seemed more than willing to talk, so I took advantage of it. Mom and

Bree were taking naps, so it was only Mike, Tony, and me in the living room.

"I want to talk to you some more about Hans Goober," I said.

"I know you think he's innocent, but I'm sure Holderman will work through the details and get to the truth."

"I'm sure he will, but I'm also sure he might take his time doing it. In the meantime, poor Hans is in the slammer."

Mike raised a brow. "I thought you barely knew the guy."

"I do barely know him, but that doesn't mean I don't care about an innocent man spending the holiday in jail. I have a plate all made up for him. Extra gravy and everything."

Mike let out a long sigh. "Okay. So what do you want to know?"

"On the surface, it appears Doug Peterson was at the house on Friday afternoon to clean it. He finished at some time prior to eight, when he went into town. He ate and had a drink, then came back to the house for some reason. Tom Flanders from across the lake said he saw his truck here at around ten, then went to visit Hans Goober. I find it odd that he didn't mention that the first time we spoke to him."

"Maybe he forgot, or maybe he had no reason to suspect Goober, so he didn't bring it up."

"Maybe. But there are other things that don't fit. We know Peterson was shot, yet not a single person at the lake has mentioned hearing a gunshot. The only two explanations I can come up with for that is that either he was shot elsewhere and brought to the lake, or he was shot with a gun with a silencer. I doubt

Hans Goober has a gun like that. I also doubt an old man who can't weigh more than a hundred and forty pounds shot Peterman, a large man weighing at least one eighty, somewhere other than the place his body was found, then carried him to the lakeshore."

Mike frowned. "Okay. Those are both good points."

"Add to that the overall timeline. If Goober shot Peterman on Friday night and found a way to dump him in the lake, why didn't anyone find the body until we did on Sunday afternoon?"

Mike's expression grew thoughtful.

"For that matter, how did Tom Flanders even see Doug Peterman visiting Hans Goober on Friday evening? Yes, he has a telescope that I'm sure he uses to spy on this house, but it was pitch black outside on Friday at ten p.m. And it isn't like spying on this house, with all the interior lights on. There aren't any lights between this house and Goober's."

"What are you saying?"

"I'm saying Hans Goober is innocent. Someone else has to have shot Peterman."

"Okay, who?"

I paused to think about that. Who made the best suspect? "Tom Flanders."

Mike looked doubtful.

"Think about it. He's the one who made a big fuss about the Techucom folks. He said he could see their comings and goings through his telescope, which I believe, also might justify his statement that he saw Peterman show up and then go to visit Goober on Friday night, but as we just established, he couldn't really have seen where he went after he left this house. And then there's the timeline. According to

Flanders, Peterman came back here after he left for the day, but why? As far as I know, Flanders is the only one claiming to have seen Peterman's truck here, which, as we know, wasn't here the next day."

"Maybe Peterman didn't come back to the lake to come here but to visit Hans Goober," Mike suggested.

"Flanders specifically said he saw Peterman's truck parked here. If Peterman came back to the lake to see Hans Goober, why would he park here? The road goes right up to Goober's place, just like it loops around to all the other cabins. Why not just park there?"

Mike sat back in his chair. "Good point."

"It seems to me that Flanders has been trying to divert attention from himself from the beginning. First, he pointed us to the Techucom group, and then he pointed Holderman to Hans Goober."

"So why would he kill Doug Peterman?"

I frowned. "I'm not sure."

"It seems the fact that Peterman's truck hasn't been found is a big part of this," Tony said.

"The truck has been found," Mike informed us. "I'm sorry; I thought I told you. It was found sitting on the side of the road in a residential neighborhood about a mile from town. Holderman suspects the killer drove it into town from the lake and left it there."

"A mile from town? If Doug Peterman did return to the lake that night, why would the killer drive it all the way back to town? Did the crime scene guys pick up any physical evidence?"

"Holderman has the lab working on it. Look, Tess, I know you're concerned about the old man, but it's Thanksgiving. Why don't you let Holderman do his job so you can enjoy this time with the family?"

"But…"

"Even if Goober didn't kill Doug Peterman, he was part of a scam to sell maps to ten clueless city folks who were probably led to believe there really is a treasure."

"There might be one, and Hans Goober never said the ten people were told they were buying the exclusive rights to the map. Are you saying he broke any laws?"

Mike shrugged. "Maybe not."

I looked out the window. The snow had stopped, at least for the moment. "I could use some air. I think I'll take a walk." I looked at Tony, who mostly had been sitting quietly since my conversation with Mike began. "Do you want to come along?"

"Sure. I'll get our coats."

"And Tess…" Mike said. "Don't go bugging Tom Flanders. All you have is a very weak theory. Give the man a break. It's Thanksgiving."

"Don't worry. He's not home. He's spending the day with Conrad Bilson and his daughter."

After we left the house, Tony asked the question I expected. "So what's really going on? Why the walk?"

"Mike is tired and just a bit tipsy. Which is fine. It's been a tough week for him, and this is supposed to be his vacation. But he isn't going to be any help right now. I need to think. The more I think about it, the more certain I am that Tom Flanders could be the guy."

"I agree it seems like he's been providing information to lead suspicion away from himself, but why would he kill Peterman?"

"I don't know." I began to walk faster. "I think we need to go back to the beginning."

"Okay." Tony grabbed my hand. "But let's slow down a bit."

I slowed my pace and took a deep breath. "Let's go back to when we found the body at the lake on Sunday afternoon. I know Mike said it looked as if he had been dead a day or two, which would make it possible for him to have been shot on Friday night, but it doesn't seem likely he'd been floating in the lake for two days. Yes, it's winter, and there aren't a lot of folks spending time at or around the water, but it seems in two days' time someone would have seen him."

"So maybe he was killed on Friday night or Saturday morning but not dumped into the lake right away."

"For that to happen, someone would have had to have somewhere to keep him. If someone like Hans Goober shot him on Friday night, it seems unlikely he could have hidden the body only to move it later. As I pointed out, it seems unlikely Goober could have moved him at all."

I chewed on my lower lip as I continued to walk. Walking and thinking seemed to go together. "Do you remember if anyone other than Tom Flanders mentioned seeing Peterman return to the lake on Friday night?"

Tony didn't answer right away. "No," he finally answered. "I don't think so. It was Flanders who first said he saw the truck at the house at around ten p.m., and it was he who told Holderman he saw him go to Goober's cabin that same night."

"Okay, so what if Peterman never came back to the lake? Say he picked up the key on Friday afternoon, came out to the house and cleaned it, then went into town for his dinner and drink. What if after leaving the bar he went somewhere else? What if he went to see someone who lived in the area where his truck was found?"

"If that was so and you think Flanders killed him, how would he even know he was there?" Tony asked.

"Flanders could have seen him at the bar and followed him, or…" My eyes grew wide. "Or," I said as a new realization gripped me, "Peterman went to see his mistress after he left the bar and Flanders just happened to run into him there."

Tony's eyes grew large as well. "You think Peterman was having an affair with Flanders's ex?"

"Maybe. If Flanders wasn't really over her, he could conceivably have decided to stop by, or even just driven past her place. He saw Peterson's truck there, so he waited for him to come out, then grabbed him and took him somewhere isolated and shot him. I don't know where, or whether he kept him somewhere before he shot him, but I do think he probably didn't dump him in the lake until Sunday."

"That all makes sense. We need to call Holderman. If Tom Flanders is the jealous sort and he did find Doug Peterman and his ex-wife together, Doug might not be the only one on whom he took out his rage."

After we returned to the house, I called Officer Holderman and explained my theory. He agreed to check on Tom Flanders's ex and then to stop by

Conrad's daughter's to have a chat with Flanders as well. All we had to do was wait.

God, I hated waiting.

Chapter 12

Friday, November 23

"Oh, this one is perfect." Bree clasped her hands together as she turned toward Mike, who carried the ax.

"You're sure? Once I cut into this little tree, it's yours."

"I'm sure," Bree said as she stepped aside to give Mike the room he'd need to cut down the tree we'd spent almost two hours selecting. "It's tall but not too tall, and it's narrow, so it won't take up a lot of space. It has sturdy branches that are nicely spaced for the ornaments I plan to decorate with. It really is perfect."

"Okay." Mike swung back the ax, then met the trunk of the tree with the full force of his body.

It did my heart good to see Bree so happy. I mean really happy. She hadn't always been lucky in love. In fact, up until she began dating Mike, her love life had been something of a disaster. But I could see she was great for Mike and Mike was great for her. I was sure this was the first of many Thanksgivings we'd all spend together.

"You know, maybe as long as we're out here, I'll go ahead and get one for the restaurant," Mom said. "Just a small one. No more than five feet. And narrow, like Bree's."

I could see Mike was about to argue, so I jumped in. "I think that's a wonderful idea, and I know just the tree."

"You do?"

"We passed it an hour or so ago, but we'll walk right by it on our way back to the house. It's a cute little silver tip and I think you'll love it."

Mom smiled. "Oh, let's do take a look. I love silver tips."

I smiled back at my mom. "I know you do. I remember walking over almost every inch of the White Eagle National Forest looking for the perfect silver tip on more than one occasion."

"How about you?" Bree asked as her tree toppled to the ground. "Do you want to get one too?"

I glanced at Tony. "No. Tony and I are going to wait to decorate the rest of his house and my cabin before we put up trees. Neither of us has a place of business to decorate, so I think we're good. Besides, I'm freezing. I'm beginning to dream of the hot tub and a hot toddy."

"That gets my vote," Mike said, handing the ax to Bree so he could hoist up the tree onto his shoulder.

As we headed back to find the tree I was sure Mom would love, I looked back on the week that had featured so many highs and lows, I actually felt as if I had literally been riding a roller coaster. As it turned out, my theory about what had happened to Doug Peterson had been spot-on. He had been sleeping with Tom Flanders's ex. In fact, he'd been sleeping with her since before she was Tom's ex. When Flanders found them together, he was sure why his marriage had broken up. Unfortunately, the ex hadn't fared Flanders's rage any better than Peterson. Holderman had found her body in an ice fishing hut near his cabin, which was where he suspected Peterson's body had been before it was dumped in the lake. Why Flanders had decided to do that, where it was sure to be found, we'd probably never understand. It seemed like a dumb move to me, but maybe he really did think he would be able to pin the murder on someone else, which might help to divert attention away from him once someone realized his ex was missing.

Whatever the reason, the end result was that Flanders was arrested and Goober was set free. I took him two huge plates of food last night and planned to take him another one today. In a way, the fact that the murder was related to Peterson's catting around and not a government cover-up or secret treasure map seemed a bit anticlimactic, but Tony had been saying all along that the motive would end up being something fairly mundane, and he'd been right.

"I think Leonard has managed to get more snow frozen into his fur than there's left in the forest." Bree laughed.

"He does like to roll in the stuff," I said. "We'll need to dry him off and brush out the snow before we bring him in the house."

"We should get Mom's tree, then head back to get cleaned up if we still want to go to the festival in town," Mike said.

"I'd like to go," Bree said.

"Me too," I agreed. "I need to drop a plate of food off for Hans Goober first, though. I said I would." I glanced at Mom. "He loves your gravy so much, I wouldn't be surprised if he shows up at your doorstep with a proposal."

Mom laughed. "Thanks, but I think I've had my fill of men who like to hang out alone at the lake. If I marry again, it will be someone who likes to stay close to home."

I noticed Mike's mouth tighten, but he didn't say anything, so I started chatting about the wine tasting and how we might want to hire a cab to take us to and from town instead of driving. I wasn't even sure there were any cabs up here at the lake, but Tony offered to look for an Uber, and offered to be the designated driver if we couldn't find one.

******

"Mr. Goober, are you here?" I called out after knocking on his door later that afternoon. I'd waited a full minute and was about to walk away when he walked up behind me with his shotgun in one hand and something dead in a bag in the other. I decided I didn't want to know. "I see you've been hunting."

"Man's gotta eat."

"Maybe, but I brought you another plate of leftovers."

"Extra gravy?"

I smiled. "Of course."

"Well, come on in." He opened a locker that was built into his deck and put whatever was in the bag inside before opening the front door and entering the small cabin. I handed him the plate of food. He licked his lips as he looked at the contents.

"We'll be leaving tomorrow. I thought I'd pack up whatever leftovers we have and bring them to you. If you have room in your refrigerator, that is."

"I'll make room. Your mama can cook."

"She owns a restaurant at home, so she gets a lot of practice. If you're ever in White Eagle, you should stop by. It's called Sisters' Diner."

"For more of these potatoes and gravy, I just might make the trip."

I glanced at my phone. "I really should go. The family's waiting on me to head into town. I'll be back with the rest tomorrow. Maybe at around ten."

"Ten will work. I'll clean out my refrigerator today."

I turned to leave.

"Listen, before you go, I wanted to thank you for believing I was innocent of killing Doug, and for figuring out who the real killer was."

"I was happy to help. Nothing bugs me more than an unsolved murder. Actually, I'm not a fan of an unsolved mystery of any sort."

He grunted. I wasn't sure what that meant, but it seemed friendly enough.

"You're a lot like him, you know."

I paused. "A lot like who?"

"Your father. He was a good guy and a good friend to Finn. Nearly killed him when Finn was shot dead. I don't know everything that went on at the

147

time, but it seemed as if he blamed himself somehow."

"Conrad Bilson said the same thing."

"It was a sad time for everyone here. Finn was a real popular guy, and we all looked forward to Tuck's annual visits. I heard Tuck died, but I think he really didn't."

I frowned. "Why do you say that?"

"Saw him a while back. He was having a drink at a bar on Highway 90 just outside of Butte. Thought I saw a ghost, but I didn't figure ghosts frequented bars, so I went up to him and said hi. Tuck looked as surprised to see me as I'd been to see him. I asked about what had happened to him, and he said it was complicated. He asked me not to say anything and I didn't, until now."

"How long ago was that?"

"I guess it might have been the summer before last."

"Was he alone?"

He nodded. "He was sitting at the bar next to a man who was nursing a drink, but they didn't seem to be together, although they did leave at the same time, so maybe."

"Did he say anything else?" I wondered.

"Nope. Like I said, he didn't seem real happy to see me. Anyway, I wanted you to know."

"Thank you. I appreciate that."

When I returned to the house, the others were ready and waiting for me. I plastered on a smile and launched into a conversation that I was certain would convince everyone other than Tony, perhaps, that a Christmas festival was the only thing on my mind. We hadn't been able to hire a car, so Tony was driving. He was happy to play chauffeur so the rest of us could taste as much wine as we wanted.

I hadn't been sure what to expect when I agreed to this first family vacation including Tony and Bree, but I'd actually had a good time. In a way, it was almost like Dad was there. Maybe not in person, but in spirit. Mom had wanted to come to the lake to find answers for unresolved questions, and I wasn't sure she'd found them, but she seemed happy, the smile on her face authentic. Who knew, maybe we'd started a new Thomas family tradition of a week at the lake at Thanksgiving. Or maybe we hadn't, but this week was one I'd always remember.

Chapter 13

Monday, November 26

"Morning, Hap."

"Mornin', Tess, Tilly. How was your trip?"

"Eventful."

"Eventful good or eventful bad?"

"Both, actually. I had a nice time, but I'm happy to be back. It looks like you have your Christmas display up."

"I have a whole lotta new gadgets if you're looking for mechanical reindeer or twinkling tree lights that change color."

I wrinkled my nose. "I don't think I'm in to the flash, but maybe some white lights for the tree to replace the ones the kittens destroyed last year. Oh, and some red balls. I'm hoping Tang and Tinder are old enough to leave the tree with some dignity this year."

"I heard Mike adopted a pup."

I nodded. "Leonard. He sure is a cute little guy. Sort of a handful right now, but trainable. And Mike adores him, as does Bree. It's like a Christmas miracle."

Hap chuckled. "Yeah, neither Mike nor Bree strikes me as the puppy type. I'm glad to hear things are working out."

"How are you getting along with Bruiser?" Bruiser was Hattie's dog. He hadn't liked Hap at all when Hattie first adopted him.

"I think we've come to an understanding. I bring him treats and he doesn't bite me. We both love Hattie, so we have that in common."

"I'm really happy to hear that." I glanced at the clock. "I need to get going, but I'll drop by at the end of the day and pick out some lights and bulbs for my tree. I know if I don't do it today, I'll get busy and forget about it and everything you have will get picked over."

"I'll set some things aside for you. Is Tony going to need lights as well?"

"Yeah. The kittens did a number on his tree last year too. Hopefully, whatever we buy now will survive."

I chatted with Hap for a few more minutes, then continued on my route. It seemed most of the town had gotten busy over the weekend to put up lights and decorations along Main Street. I really love this time of year. Everything somehow seems brighter and happier. It's during these winter evenings when I look back and remember the magic that can be found during the holiday season.

As he'd promised, Tony was mostly off work until after the first of the year. He was staying at my place during the week, then we'd stay at his place Friday through Sunday. Tonight, we planned to dig in and start decorating the cabin. It wasn't very large, so it wouldn't require a lot of decorations, but I was excited for us to spend our first Christmas as a couple. Tony had talked to Shaggy about the dinner party, which I found I was a bit nervous about.

"Morning, Aunt Ruthie," I greeted after entering Sisters' Diner.

"Morning, Tess; Tilly."

"I hear congratulations are in order."

Ruthie grinned. "I can't tell you how excited I am to be having another grandbaby. I had such a good time with the family over the holiday. It really reminded me of the importance of making time for those you love."

I nodded toward the back wall, where a flattened outline of the globe had been drawn. "I see you're doing your Christmas cards from around the world again."

Ruthie nodded. "It was a huge success last year."

I reached into my bag and pulled out a pile of mail that included at least ten cards. "It looks like you have a good start this year." I looked around the room. "Where's Mom?"

Ruthie tossed the pile of mail on the counter. "She ran down to the home furnishing store to see if the new ornaments were in. You know if you don't get them early, they get picked over."

My eye caught one of the envelopes and I felt my heart slow. "Hap has his decorations out," I said as I slowly nudged the top envelope from the mail Ruthie had tossed on the counter aside.

"Hap's is a good place to get lights and whatnot, but he doesn't have the specialty items we're hoping to find."

"True. I should get going. Do you have outgoing mail?"

"We do. Hang on and I'll get it."

I picked up the second envelope down in the stack I had given to Ruthie. It was postmarked from Norway. I gasped when the return address indicated that the sender was no other than Jared Collins.

"Are you okay?" Ruthie asked as she returned.

I waved the envelope. "Look. Norway."

Ruthie's face lit up. "Oh good. Our first international card." She looked at the postmark. "Oh look: it's from your mom's pen pal."

"Pen pal?" I croaked.

"Ruthie nodded. "Jared Collins. I'm sure your mom must have mentioned him. They've been pen pals since before you were born."

Okay, what? My mom had stayed in touch with Jared Collins? I distinctly remembered her saying that while she loved him and he loved her, they knew they couldn't be together, so they made a clean break. "Are you sure she's been writing to this man for that long? She never mentioned him."

Ruthie's cheeks brightened. "Perhaps I spoke out of turn. It's possible your mother might not have chosen to share her friendship with this man with her children. He was an old flame, and I suppose mothers don't discuss old flames with their children. Please don't tell her I mentioned him. Whatever they had was years and years ago."

"I won't say a word."

After I left the restaurant, I called Tony. "According to my Aunt Ruthie, my mom has continued to stay in touch with Jared Collins. She received a card at the restaurant from him today."

"Why would she lie?"

"I don't know. I know we decided to stop digging into his past—and his present, for that matter—once we realized he and my father weren't the same person."

"But now you want me to continue my search."

"I do."

"Has your mother received mail at the restaurant before from this man?"

"I don't know. The name didn't mean anything to me until recently, so I wouldn't have paid any attention. Besides, I'm not the one who sorts the mail, and I don't look through it."

"Okay. I'll dig around a bit."

"Thanks, Tony. Don't mention this to Mike. He had a hard time with everything I told him as it was. I'm afraid Mom having a pen pal who looks exactly like Dad and used to be her lover might put him over the edge."

"I won't say a thing."

I hung up the phone and headed toward the home decorating store. Ruthie had said Mom would be there, and suddenly I had an overpowering urge to ask her about the card. She was just coming out of the store with two large Christmas bags, which provided me with the perfect opportunity to try to slide my way into a conversation with her about the man I suspected she still loved.

"Here, let me help you with those."

"You have your mailbag," Mom said.

"I'm used to carrying a lot of things at once." I took one of the bags from her. "Listen, as long as I ran into you, do you think we can sit for a minute? I have something to ask you."

A look of concern crossed Mom's face. "Are you okay? Is Mike okay?"

"Everyone's fine, I promise. There's the bench in front of the furniture store. This won't take long."

"I can sit for a minute."

We reached the bench, which was back off the street and currently situated in the warm sunshine. I set my mailbag and Mom's bag at the far edge, then sat down next to her. I figured I'd jump right in. "I just delivered the mail to the restaurant," I began. "You got your first batch of Christmas cards."

"That's wonderful." Mom smiled.

"There was one from Norway with a return address from Jared Collins. Wasn't Jared Collins the name of the man you met and fell in love with right after you graduated high school?"

Mom actually blushed. "Yes. Jared Collins is the man I told you about."

"I wasn't aware you'd stayed in touch with him."

Mom hesitated. "The fact that I continued to send and receive an occasional birthday or holiday card from a man I'd once had an intimate relationship with isn't the sort of thing one shares with her children, or her husband either. Nothing inappropriate has been going on between us, but we decided after an initial clean break to stay in touch."

"And Dad never wondered who the cards were from?"

Mom hung her head. "I had a post office box when your dad was alive. After he passed, I asked Jared to send his cards to the restaurant." Mom looked up at me. "We're just friends. I haven't seen him since that trip to Norway years ago."

I took a deep breath. "Look, I don't mean to make you feel defensive. Obviously, who you correspond with is your business. But it seems like you really care about this guy. I wonder why you didn't try harder to find a way to make it work."

Mom shrugged. "It seemed too hard when we were young. Then I met your father and got married, and several years after that Jared married a woman he'd known for years. After your father passed, I thought about making a trip to Norway, but Jared was still married, so I made do with a birthday and Christmas card and an occasional chatty letter."

"And now? Is he still married?"

"His wife passed away seven months ago. I'll admit I've thought of making a trip overseas, but he needs time to mourn and I'm giving it to him."

I thought about Jared Collins and what I knew about him, including that his photo had been part of a surveillance report conducted by a private investigator working for a state senator named Galvin Kline.

"I want you to know you can talk to me about this," I said. "It isn't strange to me that you have a past or that the past you thought you left behind might at times bleed into your present."

Mom hugged me. "Thank you, sweetheart. I can't even begin to tell you how much that means to me. Jared, my feelings for him, and his presence in my life, haven't been easy secrets to keep."

"Dad is gone and Mike and I are adults now. The need for secrets is past. I love you. I want you to be happy." I stood up. "I should get back to my route."

Mom got to her feet as well.

"At the lake, you mentioned having unanswered questions. Did you find the answers you were looking for?"

Mom nodded. "I think I did."

I smiled. "Good. I had questions about Dad and his past. Maybe someday when I don't have a route to finish and you don't have a restaurant to get back to, we can talk about them."

"I'd like that."

I hugged Mom. As I stepped away, I spotted Mike coming down the street. "You might not want to mention your friendship with Jared to Mike. He has an overprotective streak when it comes to the females in his life."

"I totally agree and won't say a word. It'll be our secret."

I smiled and nodded. I supposed when we had our talk about Dad, I'd have to let her in on the fact that Mike, Bree, Tony, and I knew a huge secret about him that I was pretty sure she didn't. She might be upset and possibly even angry we'd kept it from her, but we were a family and we'd work it out, because despite anything else, working things out is what families do.

Up Next From Kathi Daley Books

Preview:

Tuesday, November 13

My name is Caitlin Hart and I am marrying the love of my life, Cody West, in exactly four days, three hours, and eleven minutes. While there appear to be a few challenges on the horizon, I am determined that nothing is going to ruin my special day. Not the major storm that's supposed to blow in by tomorrow evening, not Cody's obnoxious cousin who showed up with Cody's mother despite Cody's intentionally not inviting him, not the black eye I now sport after falling into the bedroom door after tripping over my dog Max, and not the new wedding venue I must find after St. Patrick's, the church I have attended my entire life and the church I've dreamed of getting married in since I was old enough to dream of getting married, has closed for repairs following a small fire that appears to have been caused by an electrical malfunction.

"We might have a problem," my sister, Siobhan Finnegan, said to me after she'd tentatively entered my small seaside cabin through the side door.

"Of course we do," I answered, rolling my eyes. "Did the florist come down with the plague or did the bakery burn to the ground?"

"Worse."

"What can be worse than a bakery burning to the ground?"

"The bakery owner, Sally Enderling, was found dead this morning by her assistant."

I placed my hand on my heart. "Oh no. I'm so sorry. What happened?"

"I spoke to Finn," Siobhan referred to her husband, Deputy Ryan Finnegan. "It looks like someone came up behind her and hit her with an object they believe, based on the size and shape of the wound, was a rolling pin. She was found facedown in the walk-in refrigerator."

"That's awful. The poor woman. I can't imagine who would do such a thing." I didn't know Sally well, although we did run into each other from time to time, and she seemed nice enough. She'd moved to the island four years ago from Seattle, but once she settled in, she jumped right into public service by running for a board position with the local chamber of commerce. She'd done a bang-up job, from what I understood, and there was even talk of her running for a seat on the town council in an upcoming election. I knew she was married to an accountant who had an office in Seattle but had arranged to work remotely a good deal of the time. I couldn't imagine who would want to harm the woman. "Are there any suspects?"

"One," Siobhan said. I couldn't help but notice that she seemed to be cringing as she spoke. "It seems, based on what we know at this moment, the last person to see Sally alive was Cody's mother."

I closed my eyes, took a deep breath, and blew it out slowly. "Cody's mother?"

Siobhan nodded. "That's what Finn said. According to Sally's assistant, Carla, Cody's mother went to see Sally yesterday afternoon shortly before closing."

"Why would Mrs. West go to see Sally?"

"It seems she wasn't a fan of the plain white cake you chose, so she decided to speak to Sally about adding a different filling to each layer. Sally very nicely informed her that you'd specifically requested a simple frosting, and that you'd stated quite clearly that you didn't want filling of any flavor, at which point Cody's mother started yelling at her."

I slowly counted to ten before continuing in a much sterner voice than I'd intended. "Why on earth would Mrs. West yell at Sally?"

Siobhan crossed her arms over her chest. "Hey, don't shoot the messenger."

I closed my eyes and blew out a breath. "I'm sorry. It's not your fault. I didn't mean to shout. Go on."

"Carla had to pick up her daughter from dance class, so she left in the middle of the conversation, but based on what Carla told Finn, Cody's mother was very forcefully pointing out that she would be the one paying for the cake, which made *her* the customer, which in her mind required Sally to make the changes she was requesting."

I tossed back my head and threw up my arms. "That woman insisted on paying for the cake. I never asked her to contribute a dime to this wedding, but she showed up a week before she was scheduled to arrive with Cody's totally irritating cousin in tow and started making demands. Paying for the cake was one of those demands."

Siobhan took my hand in hers. "I know, sweetie. And you've done such a good job of sucking it up and allowing her to participate. I don't think the cake or the filling or the fact that Cody's mom seems to be torturing you for not having the wedding in Florida is the point of this conversation, however. The point is that Mrs. West threatened to hurt Sally, and now she's dead."

"She threatened to hurt her?" I screeched.

Siobhan nodded. "Two women who were passing by the bakery told Finn that Mrs. West insisted Sally make the changes she wanted or suffer the consequences. I suppose she could have meant many things by that, but the sheriff is taking her threat seriously. Finn said he's on his way to the island to question her himself. Finn's been instructed to bring her in."

I fell back into a chair, which, fortunately, was directly behind me. That was it. God was definitely sending me a sign that I wasn't supposed to marry Cody. There really was no other explanation. "So Sally died yesterday afternoon?"

"Finn thinks so. He's waiting for the medical examiner to say exactly when she died, but Carla said Sally had on the same clothes she'd worn the day before today, and it didn't appear she ever went home."

"Wouldn't her husband know that for certain?"

"He was in Virginia visiting his mother, who's been ill. No one realized Sally hadn't gone home until Carla showed up for work this morning."

I took several deep breaths as I tried to steady my suddenly very shaky nerves. "Does Cody know?"

"Finn was going to track him down and talk to him right after he hung up with me."

This wasn't going to go over well at all. "He went to the north shore this afternoon to take some photos for the story on the fire at the old community church. I doubt he's back yet. Still, he should be available by cell." I stood up and took yet another breath to strengthen my resolve. "I suppose I should head over to Finn's office."

"Finn said no. He was going to explain things to Mrs. West when he picked her up. He'll call after she speaks to the sheriff, but he didn't want you anywhere near the office when he speaks to her. I think all we can do is wait."

Well, that was just fantastic. There was nothing I liked better than waiting on the sidelines while the world crumbled around me.

"Cait? Are you okay?" Siobhan asked when I didn't answer.

I nodded. "I'm fine. I trust Finn. I'm sure he has everything under control." I glanced at my dog. "I think I'm going to take Max for a run."

******

Later that afternoon, I decided waiting was for the birds and headed to the newspaper to see how Cody was doing. Finn didn't want me anywhere near his office while the sheriff was on the island, but the newspaper was all the way next door, so I was sure it would be fine.

It wasn't.

After being scolded by Finn about following directions and actions having consequences and a whole bunch of other malarkey, I decided to go down the street to Coffee Cat Books, where I knew I would find people who loved me *and* wouldn't yell at me.

"Cait, what are you doing here?" My best friend and maid of honor Tara O'Brian asked. "I thought you were taking the day off to work on wedding stuff."

"I was, but then the woman making my wedding cake was murdered and Cody's mother is the prime suspect, so I decided angsting over a new venue could wait."

Tara's mouth fell open. "What?"

I walked into the cat lounge and flopped onto the sofa. Tara, my sister Cassie, and our assistant, Willow, all followed. The three women stood staring at me like I'd lost my mind. Who knew, maybe I had.

"Maybe you should start at the beginning," Tara said.

I nodded. "I was at the cabin late this morning, trying to figure out what I was going to do about the ceremony, now that the church is closed for repair, when Siobhan came over to let me know she'd spoken to Finn, who'd informed her that Sally from the bakery had been found dead by her assistant this morning."

"Oh no. Poor Sally," Willow said. "What happened?"

"She was hit from behind with a rolling pin or a rolling-pin-shaped object. At least that's what Finn suspected."

"So get back to the part about Mrs. West," Cassie suggested.

"Finn told Siobhan it appeared as if Cody's mother might have been the last person to see Sally alive. It seems she went to the bakery late yesterday afternoon to change my cake order because, apparently, white cake with white frosting is boring and stupid."

I saw Tara cringe.

"Sorry." I cringed in response. "That was rude and very inappropriate. A woman is dead and here I am, complaining about the actions of the woman who might have killed her."

"Mrs. West might have killed her?" Tara asked, taking a seat next to Willow.

"Finn said two women were passing the bakery while Mrs. West was yelling at Sally. They heard her tell Sally to make the changes or suffer the consequences."

Willow audibly gasped. "You don't think she actually…"

"No. At least, I hope not. But the sheriff is taking the threat seriously. He told Finn to bring Mrs. West in for questioning. I think she's still there. I was told to stay far away from the place while the sheriff's on the island. And I did. For a while. But I got tired of waiting, so I decided to go by to take a peek. Finn saw me and yelled at me, so I came here."

"You know Sally was Sheriff Fowler's half sister?" Willow asked.

I frowned. "She was? I had no idea." I bit my lip. "I guess that's why Finn wanted me to stay out of the line of fire. He was just looking out for me."

"She and her husband moved to the island from Seattle to be closer to him," Willow confirmed. "I attend the same exercise class as Sally, and while I wouldn't say we were close, we chatted on several occasions. It sounds like Sally and her brother were pretty close."

"This sounds really bad," Tara said.

I had to agree.

"The sheriff must be devastated," Cassie said, a touch of sadness in her voice.

"Yeah," I agreed, feeling like a terrible person for trying to make Sally's death all about me.

"Do you think they're going to put Mrs. West in jail?" Cassie asked.

I narrowed my gaze. "I don't think based on an argument and nothing more they would actually arrest her."

"What if there's something more than just the argument?" Willow asked.

I really, really wished I could say without a doubt in my mind that Cody's mother would never get mad enough to haul off and smack someone with a rolling pin, but from her behavior in the past few days, I couldn't help but wonder if that wasn't exactly what she'd done.

******

While Sheriff Fowler didn't arrest Cody's mother, he did tell her that she was a person of interest in the investigation and warned her not to leave the island, which she wasn't planning to do anyway. His request still angered her. When Cody arrived at my cabin after dropping his mother at her hotel, he looked as if he'd been put though the ringer. Poor guy. I couldn't imagine how I'd feel if my mother was the prime suspect in a murder investigation.

"Does it seem as if the sheriff actually thinks your mother is guilty of killing Sally?" I asked after opening a beer and handing it to the man I still hoped to marry in just a few days if we were able to find an alternate venue.

"He didn't say it in so many words, but Finn said in confidence that my mother was argumentative and even somewhat belligerent while being interviewed, which didn't help her case." Cody ran his hand through his hair. "I suspected my mother might not be quite as okay with our wedding plans as she indicated when I originally spoke to her. I even suspected a bit of an attitude, but I honestly didn't expect her to act the way she has."

"It does seem as if she's been trying to sabotage our wedding ever since she arrived on the island." I sighed, sitting down next to him. "I don't understand why. Doesn't she like me?"

Cody used one finger to tuck a stray strand of hair behind my ear. "She likes you. It's just that she blames you for ending my military career. I knew that and should have anticipated there was going to be fallout."

I sat up straight. "What? How can she blame me for ending your military career? I had nothing to do with that. We weren't even dating when you decided to leave the SEALs and move back to the island."

"I know." Cody let out a long breath. "It's just that she really had her heart set on my being career military, like my grandfather. And at one point I considered a career in the military as an option. But after a decade in the Navy, I realized that wasn't what I wanted for a lifetime. After moving back to the island and buying the newspaper, I had to explain my decisions to her. In the course of listing my reasons, I might have let it slip that one of them had to do with my feelings for you, and my desire to live in one place long enough to see where those feelings might lead."

I closed my eyes and groaned. And here I'd been thinking the only problem the woman had with me was my desire to get married on Madrona Island rather than in Florida. For the first time I understood that the loving, close mother-daughter relationship I'd hoped to have with Mrs. West had been doomed from the beginning.

Cody continued. "I'm sorry my mother this way. I thought she'd have the maturity to behave herself at my wedding despite of her feelings, but I can see now I was wrong. I don't believe she'd kill anyone, but I have no doubt she not only tried to sabotage our cake but that she yelled at the poor woman for hesitating to do what she demanded."

I couldn't help but throw my hands in the air. "So what do we do now? Do we cancel the wedding? For all we know, your mother could be in jail by Saturday."

"She isn't going to be in jail. We'll figure out who really killed Sally and my mother will be off the hook."

I began to pace. "We're getting married in four days. Four days!" I couldn't quite keep the screechy, loud tone out of my voice. "We don't have a venue for the ceremony or a cake. Your mother is not only the prime suspect in a murder investigation, but even if we manage to clear that up, she'll still hate me." I took a long breath in, then blew it out slowly. "Maybe this wedding just wasn't meant to be."

Cody put his hands on my shoulders. Turning me toward him, he looked me directly in the eye. "Are you saying you want to cancel the wedding?"

I felt my anger dissipate as I looked into Cody's deep blue eyes. "No. That isn't what I want. I want to marry you and have your babies and build a life with you, but it seems as if things shouldn't be this hard."

"I know." Cody pulled me close and wrapped his arms around me. "But sometimes life is hard, and sometimes we're forced to make compromises. I wish you'd been able to have your dream wedding. I really do. But I know we make a good team. A strong team. If we work together, I know we can figure this out."

I squeezed Cody around the middle with my arms. "You're right. I'm sorry about the meltdown." I loosened my grip and took a step back. I looked at Cody him again. "What we need is a plan. A list. We have four days to pull everything together."

Cody kissed me on the nose. "That's my girl. I'll grab a pen and pad and we'll get to work."

I sat down on the sofa and stared into the cracking fire I'd built earlier to chase away the chill. Cody and I had real obstacles to overcome if we were going to get married on Saturday as planned, but if it took every ounce of energy I had, somehow I was going to make it happen.

"We have several small obstacles and one very large one," I said once Cody sat down next to me. "Beginning with what seemed like a huge obstacle this morning and now seems like a minor problem compared to Sally's murder: We need a place to hold the ceremony."

"What about here?" Cody asked. "The reception is going to be here on the estate, so why not just do the whole thing here?"

"What about the storm? We could cram everyone into the house for the reception if need be, but there won't be room to set up chairs for as many people as we ended up inviting."

"Yeah," Cody said. "The storm could be a problem. It's supposed to roll in tomorrow evening and the first wave should blow through by Friday morning, but according to the weather forecast, there should be a second wave blowing through shortly after that. If we're going to get married on Saturday, we need an indoor venue. Maybe the recreation center?"

I made a face. "That seems cold and impersonal. What would you think about postponing the wedding?"

"Until when?" he asked.

"Father Bartholomew is still waiting for the contractor to get back to him, but he hoped the church would be repaired in time to reopen on Sunday, November 25. If that happens, he offered to let us have the ceremony after the morning services. I know that isn't ideal, but we'll need to call everyone we invited anyway, so other than your mother and cousin, who came from out of town, I'm pretty sure everyone else will be able to come on the twenty-fifth."

"And if it doesn't reopen by then?"

"Then we'll need to move on to plan B, or maybe by that point it will be plan C. I know there's quite a bit of uncertainty involved at this point, but Father Bartholomew should have a better idea when the contractor will be done by the first part of next week. I'm inclined to wait to see what he comes back with."

Cody paused. From his frown, he wasn't happy with the idea, but eventually, he admitted that postponing the wedding to see if the church could still work out might be the best idea.

"So, about the cake…" Cody said.

"I'll ask Tara to make it. I should have asked her in the first place. I didn't want to make such a huge request because she's already going to be maid of honor and she's covering for me at the bookstore, but I kind of think she was hurt when I decided to order the cake from Sally."

"Okay." Cody jotted down a few notes. "We'll ask Father Bartholomew about doing the wedding at some point after the church reopens and Tara to do the cake. Are you still thinking of having the reception here at Finn and Siobhan's place?"

I nodded. "If it turns out to be nice by the time we get around to doing the ceremony, we'll have it in the yard, and if the weather is bad, we'll all cram into the house."

"Okay. Anything else?"

"It sounds like we have it covered, although it might be a good idea to find Sally's killer so your mom is no longer a suspect and we won't have that hanging over our heads."

"Let's call Father Bartholomew, then talk to Siobhan and Tara. Once we have those details ironed out, we can focus on proving she didn't kill Sally."

"Are you sure she didn't?" I asked.

"Of course I'm sure she didn't. I know she's been acting irrationally since she's been here, but she wouldn't attack anyone. At least I don't think she would."

"Has your mother always been this domineering?"

Cody shrugged. "She's the sort of person who likes to get her way. I know that's why my dad left. I suppose it's also why I went into the military. She had it in her head that I was going to have a career in the military, and she isn't the sort of person you say no to. I think she means well, but she does have a way of steamrolling over anyone who disagrees with her."

"Have you ever witnessed her taking out her frustration in a physical manner? Could she have been so frustrated that she hauled off and hit a woman who wouldn't do as she asked before she even had a chance to think about the consequences?"

Cody frowned. "Honestly? I've seen her become physically aggressive. Not hit anyone, but she used to throw things at my dad. Dishes and knickknacks mostly." Cody groaned. "Maybe I was playing with fire to even invite her here. I'm beginning to think we should have eloped after all."

"I've been thinking the same thing."

Recipes:

Thanksgiving Leftovers

Leftover Turkey Sandwiches

Turkey Soup

Turkey Stew

Leftover Turkey Sandwiches

¼ cup mayo
½ cup leftover cranberry sauce
6 slices whole-wheat sandwich bread
¾ lb. leftover turkey
6 slices cooked bacon, cut in half
½ cup shredded cheddar cheese
Sliced red onion
lettuce
2 oz. cream cheese

Preheat oven to 350 degrees.

In a small bowl, mix mayo and cranberry sauce together. Spread cranberry mayo on all six pieces of bread.

Pile ¼ of the turkey onto two slices of bread and top with lettuce, followed by 2 slices of bacon, cheddar cheese and red onion. Place other piece of bread on top, cranberry mayo side down.

Spread middle piece of bread with one oz. of cream cheese. Top with turkey, followed by bacon, cheese, and red onion.

Place toothpicks in corners of sandwich. Place on sheet pan and bake until cheese is melted.

Turkey Soup

2 qt. chicken broth
½ lb. fresh mushrooms, chopped
1 cup finely chopped celery
1 cup shredded carrots
½ cup finely chopped onion
1 tsp. chicken bouillon granules
1 tsp. dried parsley flakes
¼ tsp. garlic powder
¼ tsp. dried thyme
¼ cup butter, cubed
¼ cup all-purpose flour
1 can (10¾ oz.) condensed cream of mushroom soup, undiluted
½ cup dry white wine or additional chicken broth
3 cups cooked wild rice
2 cups cubed cooked turkey

In a large saucepan, combine the first nine ingredients. Bring to a boil. Reduce heat; cover and simmer for 30 minutes.

In Dutch oven, melt butter; stir in flour until smooth. Gradually whisk in broth mixture. Bring to a boil; cook and stir for 2 minutes or until thickened. Whisk in soup and wine. Add rice and turkey; heat through.

Turkey Stew

⅓ cup chopped onion
¼ cup butter, cubed
⅓ cup all-purpose flour
½ tsp. salt
⅛ tsp. pepper
1 can (10½ oz.) condensed chicken broth, undiluted
¾ cup whole milk
2 cups cubed cooked turkey
1 cup cooked peas
1 cup cooked whole baby carrots
1 tube (10 oz.) refrigerated buttermilk biscuits

In a 10-in. ovenproof skillet, sauté onion in butter
until tender. Stir in the flour, salt, and pepper until
blended. Gradually add broth and milk. Bring to a
boil. Cook and stir until thickened and bubbly, about
2 minutes. Add the turkey, peas, and carrots; heat
through. Separate biscuits and arrange over the stew.

Bake at 375 degrees until biscuits are golden brown,
20–25 minutes.

Books by Kathi Daley

Come for the murder, stay for the romance.

Zoe Donovan Cozy Mystery:
Halloween Hijinks
The Trouble With Turkeys
Christmas Crazy
Cupid's Curse
Big Bunny Bump-off
Beach Blanket Barbie
Maui Madness
Derby Divas
Haunted Hamlet
Turkeys, Tuxes, and Tabbies
Christmas Cozy
Alaskan Alliance
Matrimony Meltdown
Soul Surrender
Heavenly Honeymoon
Hopscotch Homicide
Ghostly Graveyard
Santa Sleuth
Shamrock Shenanigans
Kitten Kaboodle
Costume Catastrophe
Candy Cane Caper
Holiday Hangover
Easter Escapade
Camp Carter
Trick or Treason
Reindeer Roundup
Hippity Hoppity Homicide

Firework Fiasco
Henderson House
Holiday Hostage – *December 2018*

Zimmerman Academy The New Normal
Ashton Falls Cozy Cookbook

Tj Jensen Paradise Lake Mysteries by Henery Press:

Pumpkins in Paradise
Snowmen in Paradise
Bikinis in Paradise
Christmas in Paradise
Puppies in Paradise
Halloween in Paradise
Treasure in Paradise
Fireworks in Paradise
Beaches in Paradise
Thanksgiving in Paradise – *Fall 2019*

Whales and Tails Cozy Mystery:

Romeow and Juliet
The Mad Catter
Grimm's Furry Tail
Much Ado About Felines
Legend of Tabby Hollow
Cat of Christmas Past
A Tale of Two Tabbies
The Great Catsby
Count Catula
The Cat of Christmas Present
A Winter's Tail
The Taming of the Tabby

Frankencat
The Cat of Christmas Future
Farewell to Felines
A Whisker in Time
The Catsgiving Feast – *November 2018*

Writers' Retreat Mystery:

First Case
Second Look
Third Strike
Fourth Victim
Fifth Night
Sixth Cabin
Seventh Chapter

Rescue Alaska Paranormal Mystery:

Finding Justice
Finding Answers
Finding Courage
Finding Christmas – *December 2018*

A Tess and Tilly Mystery:

The Christmas Letter
The Valentine Mystery
The Mother's Day Mishap
The Halloween House
The Thanksgiving Trip

Haunting by the Sea:
Homecoming by the Sea
Secrets by the Sea
Missing by the Sea
Christmas by the Sea – *December 2018*

The Inn at Holiday Bay:
Boxes in the Basement – *November 2018*

Sand and Sea Hawaiian Mystery:
Murder at Dolphin Bay
Murder at Sunrise Beach
Murder at the Witching Hour
Murder at Christmas
Murder at Turtle Cove
Murder at Water's Edge
Murder at Midnight

Seacliff High Mystery:
The Secret
The Curse
The Relic
The Conspiracy
The Grudge
The Shadow
The Haunting

Road to Christmas Romance:
Road to Christmas Past

USA Today best-selling author Kathi Daley lives in beautiful Lake Tahoe with her husband Ken. When she isn't writing, she likes spending time hiking the miles of desolate trails surrounding her home. She has authored more than seventy-five books in eight series, including Zoe Donovan Cozy Mysteries, Whales and Tails Island Mysteries, Sand and Sea Hawaiian Mysteries, Tj Jensen Paradise Lake Series, Writers' Retreat Southern Seashore Mysteries, Rescue Alaska Paranormal Mysteries, and Seacliff High Teen Mysteries. Find out more about her books at **www.kathidaley.com**

Stay up-to-date:

Newsletter, *The Daley Weekly*
http://eepurl.com/NRPDf
Webpage – **www.kathidaley.com**
Facebook at Kathi Daley Books –
www.facebook.com/kathidaleybooks
Kathi Daley Books Group Page –
https://www.facebook.com/groups/5695788231468 50/
E-mail – **kathidaley@kathidaley.com**
Twitter at Kathi Daley@kathidaley –
https://twitter.com/kathidaley
Amazon Author Page –
https://www.amazon.com/author/kathidaley
BookBub –
https://www.bookbub.com/authors/kathi-daley

Made in the USA
Columbia, SC
21 October 2018